*To Sand &
Happy Hil
for the great company!*

STRAY BULLET

SIMON DURINGER

Copyright © 2015 Simon Duringer

All rights reserved.

ISBN-10: 1511473754
ISBN-13: 978-1511473750

DEDICATION

To the few individuals who stick around through thick and thin and to all the world's individuals who suffer ill health, whether mental or physical. To the world's carers who work tirelessly to treat their patients.

To my readers and of course to Mum and Dad and my sons; Jonathan and Christopher.

I dedicate this book to you all.

Contents

1 – THE COMMOTION	6
2 – THE DEVIL INSIDE	12
3 – KIDNAP AND KILLING	20
4 – AMNESIA	26
5 – LADY OF THE NIGHT	36
6 – DESCENT INTO DARKNESS	47
7 – RECOLLECTIONS	54
8 – ENTRANCE TO THE UNDERWORLD	73
9 – THE DETACHMENT	89
10 – AN INSIDE JOB	105
11 – INFILTRATION	125
12 – LOVE OF AN ASSASSIN	139
13 – GOTCHA MAGAZINE	151

14 – LONG HAUL HOME	**157**
15 – CONSCIENCE	**165**
16 – PROSTITUTES OF LAW	**179**
17 – THE LAST JOB	**193**
18 – THE LETTER	**201**

1 – The Commotion

He lay on the top step. Ironically the last step, he thought, as he lay slumped against the large concrete pillar. A pillar of no consequence, at the entrance to a building that did not matter. He could be anywhere in the world for the difference it would make. The light breeze on his face seemed like a paradox, feeling the nature of it on his clean shaven face yet seemingly being unable to inhale the pure air it carried. His Armani suit appeared immaculate but for the creases from his fall and the blood on his chest. His back was buckled and involuntary convulsions tore through his body. Before now he had always been in control. This was a new experience that would not be relived. Fear, shock and adrenaline pumped through his body, and disorientation slowly took over his mind as he drifted into unconsciousness.

He hadn't seen it coming. They say, *'you never hear the sound of the weapon that launches the lead that gets you'*. He could now bear testament to this fact. Harvey Walters lay slumped, his body searching for breath as he lay unaware of all around him. The screams from onlookers could be heard all around, screams of disbelief and fear; fear that they might share the same fate. That today could be the last day they would share a breakfast with their families or ride a bus to town. Sirens could be heard in the distance rushing towards the scene, responding to the call of some four minutes ago, whisking through the streets at alarming speed.

The city was full of young European students there to learn a new language, shoppers on their day off from work, all wandering aimlessly in shock at what they had seen, covering their mouths like young children who have just blasphemed. Disorientation had set in on the streets of this normally sleepy city.

Amongst the confusion, one man exited a side door which led to the flats above The Half a Nickel Tea Rooms. He turned to his right, away from the commotion and walked swiftly, yet calmly from the event. The occasional tug of his collar was the only hint that something could be wrong. He passed the Halifax Bank and onto the high street almost as if a prior engagement had his mind preoccupied and making him completely unaware of the commotion that surrounded him.

Briefcase in hand, he appeared to be a man not dissimilar to any other, and within two hundred yards had blended back into his surroundings, and the throngs of businessmen appearing for their long awaited lunch breaks.

Jack Shaw did not need to look back; he knew already what was happening on the Cathedral Green. But he was angry. His teeth gritted as he thought about the events of the last couple of hours. He marched down Fore Street towards the river where he would lose the briefcase containing his dismantled rifle. He only ever used it once so few links to his personal expertise would be left behind. He was beating himself up. It should never have happened. Joe Collier was a shift worker and should not have been home for hours, but at the crucial moment, he entered his flat. A muted shot was heard in the room but no further as Jack swung around to deal with his uninvited visitor. He was quick and merciless, an outstanding marksman, but unable to take aim, he shot from the hip.

"What the fuck?" was all that Joe could muster before he hit the ground.

Jack swung back around to the window and then felt the pit of his stomach tighten as he saw the target being shuffled into his limousine. There would be no second shot. Joe had unwittingly saved the life of the target to his own detriment. On his way towards the door Jack gave an angry kick to the ribs of the deceased Joe Collier.

"Asshole!" he muttered under his breath and left the room.

He didn't like unforeseen events but had become accustomed to dealing with them. They never seemed to faze him, a trait which over the years had lulled him into almost believing he was invincible. He was teeming with self-confidence, whilst airing professional caution.

Jack was a very calculating man. He had to be in order to remain undetected for so many years. He would spend hour upon hour going over his plans and contingencies, and when finally reaching the ultimate plan, the sly grin that could overwhelm almost any woman he desired, would appear on his face and self-satisfaction would set in.

But today was different. The target *had* got away. He had not earned his bounty. Half now– half on completion was the deal. For £50,000 above his retainer someone wanted this guy dead pretty bad. He wondered to what extent security would be raised around this individual and, for how long, and whether it was worth pursuing for the extra hassle it would cause him. But, at the end of the day, he was a well-respected professional hit man, who on more than a couple of occasions, had even been hired by the FBI wishing to silence the odd individual. Though he had never been in *direct* contact with the Bureau, he would always leave a miry trail behind him to avoid *them* identifying him.

He saw dealing with the FBI as the ultimate game, working for them one minute and being pursued by them the next, until his services were once again required, when an eerie peace would be installed. He thought they were a joke. On the one side, involved in a huge drug bust and on the other, the apparently incinerated narcotics finding their way back onto the market, lining the pockets of corrupt officials.

Pah! Everyone's doing it, he thought. *Some of us are just better at it than others.*

Unlike most gangsters, Jack had had a good upbringing. His father had been a respected accountant and senior partner in a top London firm, his mother a devoted housewife who decorated and furnished their home in this foreign land. She had secretly missed America and hoped one day to return.

Educated in England, he was a keen athlete and competed as a youth in many sports, but school was also where he discovered his liking for soft drugs.

Jack paid a short visit to prison after being caught selling marijuana; done largely to fund his habit and because his devotion to his parents wouldn't allow him to steal from them. He often recalled the devastation his behaviour had caused the family and, after jail largely avoided drugs, apart from the odd joint at a party, keen to demonstrate to his parents that he was a rehabilitated man.

But whilst in jail, he had made several contacts, among them Lucio Lucianni; the head of a UK crime syndicate. Lucio had taken it upon himself to protect Jack from some of the more distasteful members of the prison population. He was of questionable heritage, wealthy but could only aspire to the apparent respectability of Jack's family.

More often than not, Lucio was invited to parties through fear rather than affection. It sickened him that he wasn't readily accepted into the more sought after circles. Jack had initially suspected Lucio of using him as a means to an end to get into those *right* circles, but while serving time, their friendship seemed to blossom and although Jack always waited for the hidden agenda to appear, it never seemed to... until 1982.

Two years after getting out of prison, Jack's parents suffered a horrendous car accident when returning home from a Rotarians charity night, at which his father had been the guest of honour. They had been on the receiving end of a head on collision with a jack-knifed arctic in foggy weather on the M1. His father was killed instantly and his mother, amongst other things, broke her neck. She suffered for days before eventually passing away without ever realising her dream to see her homeland again. Jack went into deep shock. He was 23 years old with no family left to speak of. He cried regularly for months.

His self-prescribed remedy was to immediately embark upon a journey of self-destructive behaviour, smoking marijuana and regularly snorting cocaine to relieve his anxiety. Emotionally he was on fire, and then it happened… his anxiety turned to anger.

2 – The Devil Inside

Lucio reached for the phone that morning, dialled his friend's number and waited for an answer.

Jack had slept in having consumed a cocktail of drink and drugs the night before. He opened his eyes and reached for the telephone.

He had taken to sleeping in his parents four poster bed in their respectably large country home, which he could not bear to sell once they had passed away. Financially, he had not been left wanting. Trusts had been set up years in advance of his parents' death to avoid death duties and the stripping of his father's wealth. He had always thought how morbid his father had been in thinking of such contingencies. Perhaps this was the seed for Jack's own skills in later life.

"Yeah who is it?" he growled, angry at having his sleep interrupted.

"Chill, Jack. It's Lucio..." came the response in a deep Italian accent.

Jack broke into a smile for the first time in weeks. "Jesus, you sound more like the godfather every time I speak to you!" A comment anyone other than a close friend of Lucio might have sorely regretted.

"Respeeeect..." Lucio purred. "Jack it's time to clean up, mourning is ov..."

"Why, you disrespectful bastard!" Jack snapped furiously, but Lucio continued as though there had been no interruption.

"...over. Jack, I'm your friend. You're snapping at the wrong guy." He paused, "I've got a job for you. It's payback time my friend. I'll be over in one hour."

Almost as an afterthought, he added, "Jack, don't take a hit today!" and calmly hung up.

Jack was slightly fazed and still disorientated from his potions the night before, but he realised that although he had got away with speaking to Lucio in that manner, he would need to tread carefully around him for a while. He climbed out of bed and staggered towards the en suite bathroom running his hands through his hair and scratching his over polluted nostrils. He looked in the mirror, only to see someone with tired eyes and almost ten years his senior staring back. Drugs had taken their toll on his twenty three year old body. *Lucio was right,* he thought regretfully, *it's time to move on.*

Lucio always turned up ten minutes early to meetings, perhaps through some paranoia of allowing his colleagues to be too ready for him. It was exactly fifty minutes later when the entourage arrived. A BMW 3.25i followed by a Bentley Turbo and then another BMW 3.25i, all black in colour, appeared like a lost funeral procession. Jack could see them from his kitchen window where he'd been preparing coffee. A nervous shudder tore through his body and the hair on the back of his neck stood to attention. Walking to the door, he wondered why Lucio had chosen not to visit alone.

As the entourage ground to a halt outside the house, four heavy set men, each wearing dark glasses and clothed in well pressed dark suits, ventured out from each of the BMW escort vehicles. Four men went straight to the Bentley, two stormed past Jack without saying a word and entered the house. One stood as a gate guard and another drifted around the outside of the house to the back garden, apparently searching for something.

The Bentley door remained closed until each of the men returned to the front of the house and gave a silent nod to the men waiting at the Bentley. One of the men then proceeded to open the rear door of the vehicle and Lucio stepped out. With two men at each shoulder, he was ushered as far as the front door.

"What's going on? You didn't need to bring these guys…" said Jack nervously.

Lucio said nothing. He entered the house leaving the goons behind and made his way to the spacious living room which he had visited many times before. Jack followed.

"…Look, I'm sorry about this morning…" Jack implored.

"Forget this morning, Jack. They're not here *for your benefit,*" he snapped looking out of the window at his entourage.

"I have a disease Jack and you're my cure. I think we both knew this day would come…" His eyes never left the window.

"Go on," responded Jack as his heart began to race.

"There is something... Someone I need you to remove for me." His eyes now leaving the window, he glanced across at Jack.

"I err wh... why me...? Why not get one of those guys to do it?" Jack stuttered startled at the suggestion, pointing out towards the emotionless goons outside.

"The person in question knows my organisation intimately and would suspect any of my employees. Besides Jack, you're angry and you need to focus. I want to help exorcise the Devil inside of you." Lucio walked across the room looked Jack in the eye and reached for his shoulder. Jack stood spellbound for what seemed like hours but was in fact, merely seconds, his gaze never leaving Lucio's. He thought of the pent up anger he felt for the lorry driver who had taken his family away from him so quickly and unexpectedly. He knew he would never have a regular job. He wouldn't care for the mundane life that would entail. He didn't need a job. He was financially secure. But Lucio was right, he was still very angry and there was a debt that required repayment, a debt of honour owed to Lucio.

Whether it was the cocktail of drugs still oozing through his veins or the fear of refusing, he didn't know, but he drew a deep breath, started slowly nodding his head forward as his vocal chords created the single word that finally fought its way from his mouth...

"Okay..."

"Good." Lucio purred, never doubting the response he would get but raising his eyebrows slightly, as if surprised, at the ease of gaining his friend's agreement. "Sit down and let's talk."

Lucio and Jack started discussing how this debt was to be repaid. After a couple of hours Lucio hailed *Big Benny*, the leader of the entourage, explained that he was no longer required to wait and sent him on his way. Few people knew of the friendship between Jack and Lucio and he would feel safe in these surroundings. However, every now and then a black BMW could be seen passing on the road at the end of Jack's countryside drive, a sign that Lucio's employees were not as comfortable as he was with this arrangement. They would discreetly keep a watchful eye.

Lucio's short visit turned into a two day stay while Jack questioned Lucio thoroughly as to the facts of this task and they took time to catch up. Jack was keen to keep Lucio at his side until he completely understood what and how he would conduct the job at hand. If he was going to do this, he sure as hell wasn't going to get caught. They pored over the best methodology to be used and, as all the information came together, the first of Jack's many contingency plans was created to deal with all manner of unforeseen circumstances.

The target was a common thief known in the trade as Swifty due to the speed at which he could pick locks. He had worked for Lucio's organisation for most of his adult life but, unsatisfied with the returns, he took to stealing from his own. It was only a matter of time before it would have been noticed, but Swifty, however good with his hands, was cerebrally challenged and once it finally dawned on him that he'd gone too far and would be rumbled, he fled into hiding. Whether testament to Lucio's organisation, or perhaps the lack of Swifty's imagination, it took only a week to find him staying with his sister in Holden Hurst Road in Bournemouth.

Jack considered the former and thought wryly, perhaps if Scotland Yard had more detectives as apt as Lucio's mob, there would be far fewer unsolved crimes...

Lucio's biggest fear was that Swifty's naivety in worldly matters would lead him to the police, looking for a deal to shop the organisation bosses, rather than face the grim alternative of living his life on the run.

Surveillance was put on Swifty's sister's house and reports suggested that Swifty hadn't ventured out. It would be Jack's job to quietly gain entry acting as a delivery person and then do the merciless deed, in whatever way necessary, killing the expendable sister too if she saw him or happened to be there. Lucio emphasised that it was essential to leave no witnesses. He further concluded that as the family had bad blood in it anyway, Jack would probably be doing someone else a favour by knocking her off too. Jack had only seen this side of Lucio in jail and was surprised how composed and at ease he was. He made it sound like a trip to the grocer's.

The day of the hit was planned and came around quickly. Three of Lucio's mob came to the house to collect Jack as arranged. He recalled the lack of conversation on the first leg of the journey and had put it down to pre job nerves.

The anonymous men were to take Jack to a rendezvous with a second car at one a.m. outside Reading train station. As per the plan, within minutes of their arrival, they were met by a slightly less conspicuous motor car, a beaten up old Volvo, certainly stolen but built like a tank. *This car could probably hit a truck and come out less badly off,* thought Jack, as he swapped over from one vehicle and climbed into the rear of the other.

Jack cleared his throat before asking one of the familiar faces, "You got the stuff?"

He recognised the first man, Big Benny, aptly named due to his imposing size, sitting in the passenger seat. Benny shifted the weight of his body around to shoot a look at Jack...

"Is the pope catholic?" he replied hoarsely and sarcastically.

The driver Leo roared with laughter and Marco, Lucio's cousin, caved in to giving Jack a playful yet hard jab to the ribs... "Ho! Is the pope catholic, Jack?"

Jack winced with pain but tried to force a smile, realising he was hugely out of his depth with these neurotic goons, yet feeling intellectually superior with the thought that these individuals probably had the joint IQ of a pencil lead.

He decided to play the journey out with as little small talk as possible.

Jack was in unfamiliar territory having not been to Bournemouth before. The extent of his knowledge was that there was a large pier on the beachfront. Not much use for the task in hand and he hoped these guys were more acquainted with the area.

Leo, silent since they left Reading, had navigated them successfully onto the A33 via Basingstoke, taken the A303 to Andover through Salisbury and onto the A338 towards Ringwood. From Ringwood they would be on the final approach to their Bournemouth destination... and the beginning of a new life for Jack Shaw.

Out of the blue and for the first time since leaving Reading the silence was broken,

"Stop the car, I gotta pee!" Big Benny stated...

Leo retorted, "Benny, your bladder is the size of a pea. Can't ya wait?"

Marco sniggered at the thought of this overweight, hardened brute giving away any form of discomfort or emotion. It was three forty-five a.m. and there was no traffic on the roads.

"Okay, big guy..." said Leo "...though at this time of night you are likely to freeze your wiener off." And he pulled the car off the road.

Jack decided to take the opportunity to stretch his legs. He was unsure whether the wave of unusual body cramps he was experiencing was from sitting still for too long, or from the thought that in just under two hours, he would be a killer or the other chilling possibility that *he* himself would be a dead man.

3 – Kidnap and Killing

Stewart Wilson was not having the best week of his life. A father of four daughters and a son; he took pride in his somewhat simple life. Pride in the fact that he was a complete patriot who had seen out his national service and embarked on his life's quest to provide a humble living for his family. It hadn't been easy bringing up five children on his income but he had struggled and survived with his pride intact.

At fifty nine, he retained good fitness although his age was beginning to show. His youngest daughter Sue had married during the previous year and since that day, he had an aura of completeness about him. With the last of the children fleeing the nest, it was time for him to finally enjoy the finer things in life that, due to the pressures of parenting, had eluded him to date.

Right now though, there was something very awry with his life. A few bewildering moments two days prior had left him alone. He had not eaten or slept since, sitting by the phone as instructed by the man who had taken Jacqui from him.

He would not go to the police as he was too scared... Scared of the man's threats and scared of losing everything he had worked for... *But why?* He thought... *What can I possibly have that is so valuable to these people?* He felt so lost.

Trusted and admired for his commitment to his customers over the years, never failing to serve, never feigning illness and never avoiding his responsibilities, he had no real social life, no friends to speak of... Who could he trust with something of this magnitude? The only person like that he could think of had been taken from him. He was too proud to use his children... *To show a chink in my armour? Not likely!* He would have to bide his time and see what these hooligans wanted.

It was four thirty a.m. when the call came. Stewart nervously picked up the receiver, his hands shaking.

"Wilson?" said the muffled voice.

"Yes, who are you? What have you done with my wife?" His anxiety piercing down the phone.

"Shut up and listen and she'll be cooking your fucking tea tonight. Alright?" was the angry and impatient return.

The phone went quiet. Stewart was old school and not used to such blaspheming. He sensed intimate danger.

"You work Holden Hurst Road right?"

"Yes, that's right!" Stewart replied, confusion apparent in the tone of his voice.

"There's a no through road, with a turning place off Lytton Road. Know it?"

"Yes, but what's this about? Where is Jacqui?"

"Be there at five a.m. with your milk float and spare coveralls."

"Wait... What about Jacqui?"

"Be there at five or your wife gets it. No funny business, okay?" and with that, Big Benny put the phone down.

The blood drained from Stewart's face as he began to sense his time was running out.

Marco sat in the back of the Volvo with Jack. He reached beneath the rear of the driver's seat where he had concealed the weapons and removed a Dunlop sports bag, the type appropriate for the likes of Bjorn Borg to carry onto the Centre court at Wimbledon rather than for gangsters to carry the tools of the trade. Reaching into the bag he produced a 9mm Browning with extended barrel. Jack, who was beginning to feel the adrenaline pumping uncontrollably through his body, was naïve in his knowledge of weaponry and was simply aware that it was a *point and shoot* handgun. He could only assume, from what he had seen in movies as a youngster, that the barrel extension was actually a silencer attachment.

Lucio had let him loose with a number of handguns to see which, if any, he was capable of firing. Whilst to Jack, on that day, his weapon was simply 'a gun'. In the years to follow, he would be specific and adamant about what was supplied for his work. He would become a weapons expert and a perfectionist.

Marco handed him the weapon with two extra full magazines.

"If you need these, my friend, we are all in serious trouble," he said waving the magazines in his left hand. "The arrangements are in place. It should be a walk in the park," said Marco patting Jack's left shoulder in subtle reassurance.

"...and get the right house," interrupted Benny loudly "...ain't that a must, Leo?" Big Benny laughed making him feel better about his pea sized bladder.

Jack ignored this private joke. Maybe another time he thought. "Number twenty nine, right?" he asked looking across at Marco.

"Yeah, Jack. That's the one!"

"Okay, let's get it on," roared Leo as he indicated and turned the steering wheel and led them into Holden Hurst Road. "It's that one on the left," he continued as he approached the Lytton Road turn.

"Okay, I got it." Jack said, heart in mouth. He began thinking back to the lorry driver colliding with his parents' vehicle, bringing his hatred levels to fever pitch.

Leo turned into Lytton road and with another quick right into a no through road, the street quite deserted bar a couple of cars and, more noticeably, an agitated man in a white coat pacing by a milk float.

"That's the guy!" announced Big Benny recalling his triumph at taking a defenceless woman away from her husband. "Bruising's gone down though!" He added proudly. Benny had punched Stewart in the face whilst gaining access to his house.

All eyes were scanning windows for twitchy curtains and nosey neighbours. If any were seen, a bloody battle would probably ensue, but this night was silent and it appeared all the occupants were either asleep or away.

Leo pulled the car over to block the exit routes and wound the window down. "Okay Wilson. Get in the back!"

"Where's Jacqui? You promised!" Stewart appeared visibly worried at not seeing his wife.

"Okay, off you go, Jack." said Marco, giving Jack a fatherly wink as though sending him out to bat his first ball game.

"Get in and don't cause a commotion. You'll be with your wife soon enough!" There was a chilling side to Big Benny's voice.

Jack sat in the cab of Stewart Wilson's milk float putting on the white coat and the caterer's cap that Wilson had brought on demand. He'd now got tunnel vision. He slipped the 9mm in the coat and let off the handbrake, passing the Volvo on his right, he nodded at Marco. He never saw Stewart Wilson again.

It was about twenty minutes before Jack reappeared calmly from the house. He looked different, grey and distant, his pupils dilated and his hands shaking by his side. Moving towards the milk cart, his looks certainly did not mirror those of your cheery neighbourhood milkman, more that of a survivor from a bomb blast, disorientated yet somewhat in control.

Remaining totally focused, he climbed aboard the milk cart and considered the ghosts that he had just laid to rest... *That lorry driver would not enjoy another breath of fresh air again,* he thought, though Jack would destroy this same ghost over and over in the future.

4 – Amnesia

"Dr Stone, your patient is regaining consciousness..." called Nurse Stevens.

The light shone brightly as his eyes flickered open. Still disorientated, the room spinning in and out of focus, he could see some movement around him but blurred as it was, it put him at ease...

Either there is life after death or I'm still alive... He thought, *either way I'm glad to be somewhere.*

His vision began to clear and he could make out the figure of a doctor with a stethoscope around his neck, leaning over him. He was wearing an identification badge that read; *Dr Stone, Royal Devon & Exeter Hospital.* He tried to raise his left hand to reach the doctor but his arm barely lifted two inches off the crisp linen sheets. He inched his head sideways to see another two people; a nurse with her hair in a bundle frantically scribbling on a clipboard, and the concerned look of a mother whose child had been injured. He never could resist a girl in uniform and his gaze lingered on her for a moment before passing his stare to the man standing at her side. He was a rather gloomy man in a trench coat, a man he felt he ought to recognise but could not.

"Who are you?" His voice was hoarse and barely audible, little more than a gasp. He struggled to comprehend the amount of energy he had exerted in order to expel those three tiny words. His eyes filled with tears and once again he drifted into unconsciousness.

"Okay, doc. When do I get to speak to him?" asked the straight faced man.

"Well, officer. He is fairly stable now but he needs to regain strength. We took him out of intensive care a few hours ago officer... but we will still need to monitor him closely."

"Damn... He is one of the best close protection guys we've got... I wish they'd got the Bishop instead!"

"Ahh... Yes the shooting, I heard." added doctor Stone "What happened?"

"Nothing but problems... He is involved with the Italian Carabinieri's investigations into the Vatican's lost millions. I guess the Bishop knows more than someone is happy with... Jesus..." said Inspector Bickley cringing as he swept his brow

"Well, I guess he is no longer our problem, we flew him straight back to Italy after the incident," concluded the Inspector, knowing full well the Bishop was actually still under police protection in a safe house while investigations continued.

"It's all everyone is talking about around here! They are hailing Harvey as a local hero," replied the Doctor.

"They don't know the half of it..." stated a stern faced Inspector Bickley.

Harvey Walters had begun his career in the Met in 1980 at the age of 19. His proud mother had looked on from the stands at Middle Moor Police camp whilst her son marched out to display the skills their class had learnt during the course of initial training. She'd cried tears of joy during their final march past, as her eyes met his, and the corners of his mouth turned up in recognition of one of her proudest moments.

His upbringing hadn't been easy. She had told him that his father had died when he was a toddler, but in actual fact, he was the product of an illicit affair and though he'd not known his father, he had died much later.

Although being the *other* woman, Harvey's mother liked to believe that she had been totally satisfied with the relationship. She was always wined and dined and totally adored for years, yet she knew from the outset, that there would be no chance of marriage. However, her years of loyalty were repaid as, even in death, he had looked after her. There were caveats in his will setting up an income for her, an income that, unbeknown to her, originated as a series of lump sum investments, deceitfully labelled to appear as charitable donations.

Whilst accepting the inevitable and regardless of her belief, she *had* gone through bouts of depression where hours of loneliness and paranoia towards his marriage had left her heartbroken.

Harvey had never understood why she hadn't attempted to remarry after the apparent death of his father. Even in his later years he tried to arrange dates for her with his elder colleagues. He had no lack of volunteers as even in her fifties she exuded a somewhat majestic presence. She would attend on occasion but would always shy away from them, finding it ever more difficult to bear continuing the charade for her son.

In the early 1980's she took a downward turn metamorphosing into a state of recluse, never leaving the apparent safety of her home and regularly breaking into tears, given the slightest reminder of her past love. Harvey had offered her to move in with him and his wife Jenny and their two children, Chloe and Rob, in the hope that Jenny might become her soul mate and lift her spirits. She had of course refused on the grounds that she was not prepared to lose her independence. Even so, Jenny started making regular visits and they did indeed, become good friends. Playing with Chloe and Rob seemed to act as a good rehabilitation tool for her, giving her a new lease of life.

Harvey's first big involvement in a case had been a practical disaster. He had been involved with a large squad of detectives and was called to the scene of a horrific murder involving a small time thief and his sister in Bournemouth. The main suspect, a milkman named Stewart Wilson, had disappeared and was assumed to be still at large.

There was however, no apparent motive for the murders. The horrendous manner in which Stewart had allegedly dealt with his victims had sent shockwaves through the whole of the United Kingdom. A national manhunt was launched but he and his spouse Jacqui, whose possible involvement in the murder was never established, were never found. There was even speculation that he may have murdered his wife too and gone on the run overseas. Every lead seemed to go nowhere and to the current day the case remained unsolved.

Harvey had the unenviable pleasure of being one of the first to the scene.

He had checked in to the Waterside Hotel at seven a.m. on what had started out to be a beautiful Friday morning. The Bournemouth sea air had been a treat. Harvey was attending a seminar on criminal psychology at the hotel with his partner Greg Bickley when his pager sounded off.

"Can't hide anywhere anymore, Harv!" chuckled Greg, knowing how much Harvey hated his pager.

Harvey sneered and took his leave to go to the hotel phone.

"Aw, shit!" muttered Greg a moment later, as his own pager started bleeping at him heartlessly and, he grappled with his belt strap where the pager was innocently attached to turn off the high pitched alarm.

Seconds later, Harvey burst back into the second floor room quite out of breath.

"Greg, get your arse in gear. We are about to make history."

"Yeah! Already have by missing my breakfast," sneered Greg as he rose to his feet and lurched towards the door.

"Come on... We've got to get there before they start messing with the scene..." yelled Harvey. Greg's candour clearly bothering him.

"Okay… what have we got?"

"Double murder… I'll fill you in on the way!"

Greg's head sprang up. His piercing eyes staring at Harvey, clearly shocked at the severity of the situation.

"Jesus Harv… Let's go!"

They both sprang to their heels and without regard to anything in their path, ran through the hotel reception and out to their car.

The crime scene wasn't far from where they had been staying but, as Greg climbed into the passenger seat through force of habit, he turned on the car radio system and attempted to establish which incident channel number information was being passed from police headquarters to *all available officers*. Most of the force was already on high alert, and for several hours, random stopping of innocent travellers would become almost routine as descriptions of the suspects were distributed across the network and the force searched for leads.

As they drew close to the house, blue lights could be seen all over the place. Cordons were in place for a hundred yards either side of the normally busy road.

"That'll cause merry hell for some traffic cop," Greg said in sympathy for the PC.

"No kidding," replied Harvey.

Harvey pulled up at the cordon and wound down his window "DC Walters and DI Bickley," he said holding up their identification.

"Okay sir. Park just over there and walk up," he said, pointing to a space on the other side of the road. "We are still waiting for forensics to arrive. I hear it's messy, sir…"

"Thanks," said Harvey nodding grimly.

They parked the car and walked across to the house where they found a very pale police constable standing at the front door, looking as though he had recently vomited.

"Did you find the bodies?" asked Greg.

"Yes, sir…" replied the PC with which he clutched his stomach and ran to the garden fence to wretch once again. Harvey looked at Greg.

"Are you ready for this?"

"Come on, let's get it over with," replied Greg.

Harvey opened the door and edged in. The first thing that caught his eye was the toppled side table in the hall beside which were the fragmented remains of a china vase. Directly ahead were the stairs. Harvey motioned Greg to go up them while he would search the downstairs rooms. He reached into his pocket and retrieved a set of surgical gloves, stretching them over his already well-worn hands, he reached to open the door.

The refreshing scent of Bournemouth sea air was instantly consumed by a foul overwhelming stench of rot. He turned his head sharply putting his hand over his face, pausing momentarily in an attempt to acclimatise himself before proceeding. As he walked carefully into the room the sight was bizarre. He'd never witnessed so much blood.

The room was darkened with the curtains still drawn, the overwhelming smell making Harvey wince. His foot brushed the bottom of the sofa and a swarm of blue bottle flies took flight.

Aargh! Was the noise he produced as he swiped at these parasites aimlessly.

"You okay?" Greg called from upstairs.

"Yeah..." lied Harvey, his heart rate accelerating furiously.

With the flies dispersing, Harvey bent down to take a closer look at what they had found so interesting. Squinting in the darkness he lurched over the blood strewn sofa but saw nothing... *must just be the blood...* he thought.

Looking around further, there was a grand old fire place with a large mantel piece, the centre piece of the room. His eyes were becoming accustomed to the dark now. He could see ornaments and in the centre were two bizarre mannequin heads...

"Oh no... oh my God... no..." Harvey staggered backwards tripping and knocking into a coffee table. He toppled and fell like a brick, crashing into a settee next to the entrance to the kitchen. His right hand reaching out to break his fall, making contact and sinking into something cold, his heart racing at capacity. If it got any faster he felt sure he would have burst his own blood vessels. He recovered his right hand, the blue bottles had begun a new frenzy around the room, his glove was sticky, he looked around and there it was... between the settee and the kitchen entrance was a headless torso, lying on its front, with one huge laceration from shoulder to shoulder and a pool of blood where Swifty's head had once been attached...

"Well, there's nothing up there..." announced Greg as he walked into the darkened room. "Jesus Christ..."

Harvey jumped to his feet, his cheeks beginning to swell. He pushed past Greg and ran to the front door, trying to hold in the vomit as long as possible so as not to do any *more* damage to the already compromised crime scene.

He stood at the garden fence violently vomiting for several minutes. *Gotta pull myself together*, he thought as he tried to regain his composure whilst ripping off the surgical gloves that were covered in blood from contact with the decapitated body some moments ago. He recalled the PC at the front door and was relieved he hadn't made a smart remark at the time as to his predicament. *What kind of animal are we dealing with for God's sake,* he. He jumped as he felt a hand touched his shoulder. Greg stood behind him holding out a handkerchief.

Still hunched over he sheepishly held out his hand in acceptance, feeling embarrassed at his reactions in the house.

"You okay, Harv?" asked Greg sympathetically.

"Yeah, just wasn't ready for that. Messy isn't the description I'd use to describe that scene," he continued. "Complete carnage might be more accurate. I didn't get as far as the kitchen. Anything there?" he asked, wiping his face with the handkerchief.

"Yeah, there's another body, female, with same sort of injuries," replied Greg. "Forensics have just gone up there now and the photographer is busy clicking away. You'll have to explain the lay out as you found it once we get the pictures back, okay?"

"Okay. I wonder if any pubs are open this early in the morning, I need a stiff drink!" said Harvey, still looking awestruck.

"C'mon, we'll get something for you back at the hotel," Greg said, helping his friend and colleague away from the scene.

5 – Lady of the Night

Jack Shaw sat in the lounge of his countryside home. He felt he had exorcised his ghosts and for the first time that he could remember, he felt at peace. His debt of honour to Lucio complete, he owed nothing to anyone. He felt free, free of the demons that haunted him since the death of his parents and free of his self-imposed moral obligations to Lucio.

He listened to Vivaldi's Four Seasons on his Hi-fi and streams of emotion tore through his body like bolts of lightning. But one thing eluded him; what would he do now?

He thought of the massacre he had carried out. *It hadn't been easy*, he thought. He recalled the rush of adrenaline that he couldn't possibly match with the narcotics available to him. Unable to operate the handgun, he had been forced to improvise, fighting his way past Swifty to the kitchen where he used the first available knife to fight off and stab both his victims repeatedly. He was about to leave the bodies for dead when Swifty gasped for air. Jack, confused and possessed with adrenaline fuelled anger, went back into the kitchen where he found a meat cleaver. With several savage hacks to the victims' bodies, he amputated their heads, this time leaving himself in no doubt they were both dead.

Whilst deviating from the plan, he nevertheless had completed the job. He sat and wondered what repercussions there might be from Lucio. But he felt a strange urge to do this again, a similar urge to that of taking his first hit of drugs, wanting to chase the dragon for that unrepeatable first high. He wondered how long someone could get away with similar crimes undetected. He felt sure that no one had really managed it many times without detection in the past, apart from maybe The Yorkshire Ripper... *but he was a pervert*, thought Jack with disgust.

His mind's eye was interrupted from this droned and psychotic state by the ringing of the phone. Jack sprung to his feet to turn the music down. *I'm not expecting any calls,* he thought... *surely it wouldn't be the police.* His mind started filling with self-doubt as he crossed the room to answer the telephone.

"Jack?" cried the voice with enthusiasm.

"Lucio. Is that you?" he replied tentatively.

"Jack, you old dog. Have you seen the paper today? You're a genius, they're pinning the whole thing on the crazy milkman! Why didn't you tell me what you were planning?" laughed Lucio, obviously delighted with the result.

"Err... I thought it was best kept until later," said Jack "...show you what I'm made of," he added boldly, having no wish to reveal his incompetence at operating the handgun.

"Well you certainly did that... even Big Benny's quaking in his boots. You earned yourself a lot of respect with my people. I need to meet with you, and soon, okay?"

"Okay, you know where I am… anytime, Lucio."

"I'll catch up with you tomorrow, eleven a.m. then?" asked Lucio.

"Okay, see you at ten fifty," Jack sarcastically retorted.

Rather surprised Lucio replied
"You old dog. Don't miss a thing do you! Until tomorrow then; Ciao!"

Jack replaced the receiver calmly, feeling that for the first time since he'd known Lucio he had retained some control over the conversation. A wry smile replaced his dead pan appearance. He turned up the volume on the hi-fi bringing Vivaldi back to life and strolled through to the kitchen to prepare dinner.

Jack was cooking a veritable feast for two that evening in celebration of his success and was running around the kitchen like a teenager conducting final preparations in advance of Lisa's arrival. Of course Lisa wasn't her real name, but that did not matter. He craved the company of another person that night.

He had met Lisa, or Lee as he had taken to calling her, at a social bash twelve months previously. He was instantly aware that she wasn't all she seemed. On the outside she was demure and could easily be mistaken for gentry. However, she was actually a high class lady of the night commanding a high price. It would cost Jack £3000.00 for her to stay the entire night, but he didn't mind. He could afford it. Besides, she was charismatic, either in love with a lot of people or a very good actress. Jack wasn't naïve in matters of the heart. He knew she was the latter. But, she was perfect for him, available on demand and rarely unable to call at his bidding. He often wondered how many clients she had but would never ask, wishing to enjoy the time he had with her, pretending that she was his.

She was due to arrive at nine o'clock. He had prepared prawn cocktails, Beef Wellington and, for dessert, avocados lavishly filled with yoghurt. He would offer Bucks Fizz upon her arrival and a spicy bottle of red wine from the Chateauneuf estate to accompany their meal. Jack had enjoyed learning how to cook and much preferred eating in rather than entertaining in restaurants. Although he'd been with many girls, he always felt they expected too much in return. Lee was uncomplicated. She arrived, Jack paid and she did the rest... but he liked to treat her, it was his way of paying the tip or making things run smoothly.

As would be expected for a business meeting, Lee was bang on time. She arrived in a new sporty car; a black Renault Fuego Turbo. Jack liked the car. It had a strange new style electric sun roof that seemed to extend the entire length of the car. Jack couldn't work out how they had designed it so that each time the mechanism concertinaed the vinyl precisely at the rear end of the car consistently and without error.

He had seen the car approaching up the drive and had strolled outside to meet Lee. Like a true gentleman, he opened the driver's door to greet her.

"Jack, darling, you are a dear," she said in her soft Sloane accent.

"It's always a pleasure, Lee." His grin broadening from ear to ear, he quietly passed her an envelope which she deposited on the passenger's seat before taking his hand to exit the car.

The envelope containing her fee would go unchecked. She had a strictly vetted clientele, and she knew for the best part her fee was a drop in the ocean.

The only person who had tried to retain her services through trickery had been a Member of Parliament, Mr Graeme Mellit. He had vastly underestimated her resolve and she went straight to the tabloids with the story. Following its inevitable publication, Mrs Mellit kept a stiff upper lip and stood by her man, but time took its toll on the couple and within six months, they were going through a bitter divorce. Lee had not encountered any problems since.

It pleased Jack that Lee was so discreet about payment. It was the one part of the experience that he felt was distasteful. After all, he could melt women with his charm without having to resort to his bank balance for company...

He helped her out of the car as the house security lights began to show her off in her full splendour. She wore a Versace satin valentine red bias cut dress with a decoratively beaded hem held up by two wafer thin shoulder straps. It was an outfit that probably cost more than tonight's fee and was complemented by a fairly ostentatious display of jewellery. The matching ruby Cartier drooped earrings and necklace were encrusted with diamonds and completed the outfit. No man's eye line could not be drawn to the strategically placed jewels that hung over her shapely figure. Jack wondered why she continued. After all she reeked of money. Maybe one day he would ask... maybe one day he would propose... maybe.

There was a sparkle in her bulging brown eyes. She swung her head allowing her well-conditioned long black hair to take its place. She looked up at Jack and smiled, her pure white teeth glistening perfectly.

He helped her from the car, swung the door shut and led her by the hand into the house.

"Come on... the drinks are on ice," Jack whispered in his finest English accent.

"Lead the way, my darling," she purred in response.

Jack led Lee through the door and to the left past the oil painting which immortalised the Shaw family, a painting his father commissioned when Jack was five. One of his first childhood memories was being made to sit still for hours as the artist wielded the tools of his trade, a veritable task for a child of that age. He looked up at the painting as he passed through the kitchen closely followed by Lee, wondering what his mother would make of her.

The table in the dining room was elegantly laid out with two silver candelabras down its length. It wasn't really a table to get romantic at due to its vast size. But it might have its uses later he thought. He then took the champagne from the ice bucket to make the drinks and Lee came up close to him, stroking his left arm...

"So, darling, what have you been getting up to? You look like you're enjoying a second wind," she whispered.

Jack smiled as he felt her breath caress the hair on the back of his neck.

"Well, I've laid a few things to rest, Lee. It's time to put the past to behind me," he replied glancing over his shoulder into her alluring eyes.

"That's wonderful, darling. I was getting worried for you."

"Really?" Jack sounded surprised, unsure whether he was listening to lip service. "You surprise me".

"Darling, I select my friends because I like to be with them."

Jack thought for a moment, hanging on her every word. *Friend? Not client?* he thought, turning to Lee and kissing her softly on the lips.

He passed her a glass of bucks fizz "Cheers, here's to tonight. May it never end," he added.

"Touché," replied Lee letting her ruby painted lips make contact with the Waterford champagne flute.

During the next hour and a half they sat and fed, sharing anecdotal stories, laughing and flirting with each other. Any onlooker might have mistaken their behaviour as honeymooning newlyweds. They were relaxed in each other's company and would have appeared inseparable. It was hard to believe Lee was currently Jack's employee.

Once the avocados had been consumed, Jack rose from his chair and started to clear the table. Lee remained expectantly at the table, a lady of the night she may be, a waitress she certainly was not. She felt awkward yet complimented by Jack's unnecessary efforts towards her and sat watching Jack longingly, wondering whether or not he might be the missing piece of her puzzle.

The dress was one thing, but Cartier was only worn for the most trusted of clients, those she held in highest regard, something that Jack would be completely oblivious of. She looked around the marvellous room. The antique furniture looked like heirlooms that had been passed through many generations. In fact, they had taken years to accumulate at vast cost by Jack's adoring mother. The glass display case was a shrine to Royal Doulton and Wedgwood statuettes, all telling their own small story. The corner cabinet, full of rare antique painted crystal glasses, far too beautiful to attach price tags to, she guessed correctly, they had been Jack's late father's contribution to the room…

"Coffee…?" asked Jack, startling Lee out of her perusals.

"Gosh, you startled me. I was just admiring the room, darling. It's simply divine. So… so homely," she said with an air of caution. She wouldn't lose sight of why she was there.

"Yes. I could not have agreed last week, but yes. I do have some very fond memories of it…" He looked around proudly. "Let's retire to the living room," he suggested, beckoning her with his hand.

Lee rose from the table, her posture that of a princess. She glided seamlessly towards Jack taking his arm and flashing her enigmatic smile at him. She held him tight and they almost merged as they found their way into the next room. The hair on the back of Jack's neck standing to attention for the second time that evening as, with his arm draped around her shoulder, he felt Lee's bosom find comfort pressing against his chest.

In the living room Jack released Lee and sank into one of the voluptuously upholstered arm chairs. He reached for the hi-fi remote control and brought his old friend Vivaldi with his Four Seasons into the atmosphere. Lee stood in front of him like a china doll, all twenty six years of her. She was slim, tanned and modestly endowed. She reached up towards her shoulders, her eyes never leaving Jack's. *Spring time* was chirping away on the hi-fi, the swirl of the violin strings had them both entranced but *she* had him truly hypnotised. Her perfectly painted nails flicked the straps from her shoulders and her gown effortlessly glided to the floor, revealing her equally exquisite silk and lace undergarments. Jack swallowed hard as *Largo e pianissimo sempre* played away sadly in the background. He reached out to touch and reassure her, his body moving towards her, his head at waist height, his tongue finding her navel. *I'll be doing the treating tonight,* he thought. Confused, she resisted him at first, but he was firm and would not take no for an answer.

He pulled her gently down onto the carpet and went to work, gently prying his tongue from her navel he moved down, removing her underwear in a single sweep of the hand, and continuing to her surprisingly damp clitoris. Spring's calming *Allegro* jumped in and she rode his tongue to the sweet sound of violins. She climaxed quickly crunching her hips into Jack's face. *Summer* had begun and he was ready for the chase. He moved on top of her and they wriggled around on the carpet for a few moments. Lee ripping at his clothes trying to remove them. She hadn't been treated this well since sixth form and she intended to make up for lost time. All went still for a moment as he inserted himself into her. He hadn't been with another girl for a while and hoped not to disappoint. He gained the dominant position and as the violins exploded so did they, almost becoming the subject of the music. Jack was exhilarated as *summer* took hold. His emotions hit fever pitch, biting at her neck. In turn, her nails almost pierced the skin of his buttocks. She wailed with excitement. Having already climaxed once she awaited the next with exhilaration and enthusiasm. They rolled quite violently, hitting a lamp off the coffee table and sweeping anything and everything out of their way, riding each other as though it was the last thing they would ever accomplish in life, as though their lives depended on it, clinging to each other neither gave an inch for separation, stretching all parts of their bodies. Lee tugged at his buttocks refusing to believe there wasn't more to have, Jack bucking like a mule until they reached summer's *Tempo impetuoso d'Estate* when the excitement of the orchestra, the build-up of the instruments, all coincided with the build up inside of Jack and Lee both.

"It's too muchhhh... It's too muchhh, aaaargh!" they wailed as they finally climaxed together...

Autumn's beautiful *Allegro* began. As Jack stared deeply into Lee's eyes he thought to himself, *this is as close to heaven as it gets*. He kissed her softly once more before easing himself off her.

The whole episode took only some twenty minutes, but the explosive encounter had taken its toll on both Jack and Lee alike. Wiping the sweat from his brow, the only words he could muster were... "Okay, you fancy that coffee now...?"

Lee looked at him in his eyes and laughed loudly.

"Jesus, darling. I was right. You are enjoying a second wind, aren't you? Can we not just go straight to bed?"

"Okay, I'll race you," he replied, leaping to his feet.

Lee lunged forward to grab his leg in an attempt to slow him down as she tried to get up. He fought playfully against her as she clambered up and scrambled past him heading towards the stairs. Half-heartedly he made chase, enjoying the sight of her in her natural state still looking graceful even in flight up the stairs. He roared at her playfully in chase and without looking back, she shrieked in response, running across the landing and bursting through the door of the master bedroom. She threw herself onto the bed reaching for the covers and adopting a defensive foetal position whilst waiting for his entrance. A moment later he was in the room and on top of her, tugging at the sheets, trying to get under the bedclothes with her, both laughing with delight, she eventually conceded allowing him entry. Their eyes met and once again they embraced, beginning what would turn out to be a sustained night of passion, unworthy of the seedy undertones that surrounded it.

6 – Descent into Darkness

Birds began to sing and light shone through the curtains of the master bedroom. Jack opened his eyes and glanced longingly at Lee lying beside him.

He stretched his aching muscles before manoeuvring quietly out of the bed so as not to disturb her. He headed towards the door, on the back of which hung his large towelling dressing gown, embroidered with the words Lainston House; a hotel at which he had attended a friend's wedding reception. He had worn this marvellous gown during his stay and to his surprise, upon returning home and unpacking, there it was. He smiled as he put the gown on thinking back to how mischievous he had felt at the time; how he had dodged past the reception desk looking sternly ahead wishing to catch nobody's eye in case they could read the guilt on his face. He had felt like a smuggler. He never heard from the hotel again but had received a lecture from his father on how... *The theft of towels from hotels is one of their largest single expenses, without which their tariffs would be substantially reduced.* He smirked recalling his father's stern words.

Before he left the room Lee began to stir.

"Are you going to shower, Lee?" he asked, opening the door.

"Oh I better had. Yes." Her bleary eyes meeting his, her hair resembling that of a thatched roof on a beautiful country cottage, she mustered a disorientated smile. Jack laughed,

"I know you're probably busy, but you are welcome to sleep in for a bit if you want."

"No, darling. I have things to do, I'd better get up."

"Okay. Well I'm going to get some breakfast. Do you fancy a Full English, to get those energy levels back up?" Jack sniggered.

"Sounds delightful. I'll be down in a moment… once I've showered," she replied, her voice croaking slightly as she attempted to wake properly.

Jack was feeling highly invigorated. There was a bounce in his step as he made his way down to the kitchen to prepare breakfast, almost although his psychotic actions of the previous day had never taken place.

Lisa Jackson wandered into the bathroom, her slender brown legs aching from the night of passion she had just endured. She took with her a bag full of the cosmetics that held the necessary equipment to return her to her full splendour, although it wouldn't take much as she was naturally beautiful. She turned on the shower and climbed into the cubicle, the warm water beating on her skin, she began returning to the land of the living.

Her life hadn't always been this way. Her upbringing had been modest, but comfortable. She had acquired a scholarship to gain entry to a reputable boarding school in Somerset, without which her parents she would not have been able to afford the fees. Her grades had been good enough for entrance into university, where she secretly began escorting men to complement her pitiful grant. She had planned to carry on doing this work until completion of her degree in Arts & Literature when she would return her life to normality. However, it soon became apparent to her that men were prepared to pay a lot more than the £100.00 she received for a night's work, if she was prepared to offer more than simply companionship over dinner.

Of course she had dismissed the advances at first, but after twelve months or so, she found herself escorting a handsome and wealthy businessman around London. Towards the close of the evening, he expressed a desire to take things further and although playfully at first, they began debating what would be an acceptable price.

"Darling you simply could not possibly afford me..." she had said in conclusion.

"Try me!" was the brief and confident reply.

She thought for a moment for a figure that would make him think twice, without wishing to insult him or for him to think she was belittling his advances, after all there could be more work at risk. "Three thousand pounds." she joked.

"Done!" he said without hesitation... and later that evening the progression from escort to lady of the night began.

He had been very pleased with his night out and the word spread quickly amongst his friends, who inundated her with calls for her services. She decided from the outset that she would only ever escort the ones she found palatable after that. It didn't take long for her to realise that she was making far more money than she would ever earn from a normal career, and she soon thereafter dropped out of university…

Lisa turned off the shower and stretched out for a towel. She began dabbing herself dry as she heard a car draw near on the gravel drive. Remaining unfazed by the potential appearance of visitors, she wiped the steam covered mirror with a hand towel and started to organise her hair. She always took casual clothes with her for afterwards, so as to tone the tempo down, an indication to the client that *the date* was over. Today she had blue Levi Strauss Jeans and a white polo neck cashmere jumper. She still looked radiant.

She put the remainder of her belongings away in a small overnight bag and ventured out towards the stairs wondering what wonderful cuisine had been prepared for her. As she approached the top of the stairs, she heard voices from the hallway.

"There's ten thousand there for you Jack…"
Jack stood looking at the wedge of notes and sensed taking Lucio's money would only serve for him to descend further into darkness, the darkness of Lucio's underworld…

"I was returning a favour; I owed you. I can't accept that!" she heard Jack reply.

There was something about the visitor's voice that she recognised. She remained perched and hesitant at the top of the stairs.

"Jack, it was more than a favour. You saved me from serving at Her Majesty's pleasure, besides there's a lot more where that came from..." purred Lucio. "Interested?"

"Well I have been thinking about it and..." before Jack had a chance to politely turn down any future opportunities Lee appeared.

"Good morning, everyone. I hope I'm not interrupting. It's Mr Lucianni, isn't it?" interrupted Lee as she strutted down the staircase and into the kitchen. She held out her hand. "I'm Lisa."

Lucio looked dumbfounded for a second but quickly regained his composure.
"You may call me Lucio." he purred, suspiciously looking to Jack for an explanation. "Jack this must be your best guarded secret." Jack blushed.

"Lucio this is my friend Lee. She stayed over last night." He continued, "Lee, your breakfast's in the oven. I'm afraid if you'd like eggs you'll need to cook them yourself. Lucio arrived before I had a chance to..."

"Don't worry, darling. Why don't you take Lucio through to the living room and I'll bring you some coffee once I've eaten?" Lee interrupted again.

Jack hardly knew what to say, it seemed the hired whore had turned into the hired house wife!

"Err... yes that's a great idea thanks, Lee." He didn't want to give Lucio the impression he needed to hire women and so he played along.

"Shall we...?" He beckoned to Lucio, whose mind was playing overtime at how this lady might know him. They wandered through to the living room.

Lee sat in the kitchen to eat her breakfast. Her mind drifted onto what Jack and Lucio might do for a living. It was part of her code never to ask personal questions. She was surprised at Lucio's comments though. It seemed somehow Jack had kept Lucio from prison. *Maybe he is a lawyer or an accountant?* she pondered. *If so, he's one of a kind...* she thought smirking to herself.

The alarm on the coffee maker sounded and she rose to try and find the necessary porcelain to create a reasonable presentation for Jack's guest. This was not her forte, however for a first attempt she seemed quite pleased with herself.

The living room door opened and Lee strolled in with the tray. "I'm sorry, Lucio. If Jack had given me more notice I could have been more organised," she reported apologetically.

Jack, although almost speechless, was pleased at this charade and was curious to see when it would end.

"Lisa, where has Jack been hiding you?" replied Lucio, desperately searching his mind for his connection to her. She simply acknowledged the compliment but did not reply.

She had become very observant, a professional necessity, and recognised the two had been as thick as thieves when she entered but very quickly changed the subject once she approached them.

They continued talking but about nothing in particular while Lee was in the room and after ten minutes or so Lucio looked at Jack;

"Well, Jack. I need to be somewhere else. Keep me informed of your progress." He turned to Lisa. "It has been a pleasure, Lisa," he said uncomfortably.

Jack walked Lucio to his car to see him off. Lee remained in the house and observed through the kitchen window as Jack ushered Lucio into his Bentley.

Once Jack reappeared in the kitchen Lee said,
"I'm sorry, Jack, if I read too far into the situation."

"Lee…" Jack replied awkwardly "will you come back to speak candidly with me when you have time later this week?"

"You know my rules, Jack," she replied abruptly picking up her bag and starting for the door.

"Can you not break them just once?" he implored.
"No." she said as she reached the front door. She turned looking deep into Jack's eyes and smiled. "Maybe…" she said and with confusion ruling her mind, she hurried to the car and sped off down the driveway.

"Damn," muttered Jack to himself. "I think she likes me."

7 – Recollections

Harvey Walters regained consciousness having spent almost three days and nights in a coma. His first sight was that of nurse Stevens arranging flowers, sent by his wife and children that morning.

"Ah, Mr Walters. How are you feeling this morning?" she asked chirpily, the look of a concerned mother no longer so apparent.

"I'm…" He coughed hoarsely. "Do you have any water?" he mumbled, unable to continue.

"Why of course." She took the glass from his bedside table and wandered over to the sink.

"You're one lucky man," she said returning with his glass. She didn't pass him the glass, but rather put the glass to his lips allowing him to drink with her help.

"Where am I?"

"You're in the Royal Devon and Exeter Hospital. You were shot outside the Cathedral and that Italian Bishop by all accounts has already left the country." She paused "The entire population around the city thinks you are a hero for saving him!"

"What Italian Bishop?" he asked, trying to recall the events of the past few days.

"You were his bodyguard. You know your boss has spent the last two days sitting with you, eventually we had to send him home." She chuckled. "He must be some friend."

"Was he the guy in the trench coat?" A rush of fear cascaded through his body as this unfamiliar information was being fed to him.

"Oh dear," mumbled the nurse under her breath. "I think you'd better try and rest now."

"Wait, but what about…"

"Don't worry. You will have plenty of time for questions later," she said and scurried off to find Dr Stone.

Dr Stone was on an eight a.m. to eight p.m. shift. It was now nine p.m. and he would be lucky to get away by midnight. There was nothing unusual about this. With hospital overcrowding and a shortage of medical staff, most of them worked unauthorised and unpaid overtime. Nurse Stevens found him in his office trying to sneak in a break before starting his next offensive on the ever growing workload. She knocked at his door and entered.

Dr Stone was perched at his desk with head in hands wondering for how many more years he could put up with disease and death. He wore a gold watch which had been presented to him one year earlier for twenty five years of service. It had been paid for by the staff in recognition of their respect for his work. He was a caring man but was sickened at the way the National Health Service had changed over the years. Everything had become financially orientated. Caring for the sick, in his mind, had become a secondary consideration. He had given up his marriage for medicine and his only daughter was now an adult. She had foolishly he considered followed in his footsteps. *It was no life for a girl*, he thought. His home life was non-existent, as he had been unable to find a woman who could understand the long hours of work he endured, and the regular call outs from home. He longed for a woman's company.

He heard the door open and he lifted his head. Hiding his thoughts he presented the nurse with a smile.

"Nurse Stevens. What can I do for you?" He had become very fond of her during the four years since they had started working together, treating her more like a daughter than a colleague. Perhaps this was in some part through guilt at not seeing his own daughter very often over the years.

"It's Mr Walters. He's conscious but seems to have... amnesia," she said, realising he would have to officially make that diagnosis himself.

"Right, it may have been the shock... How sure are you?"

"Well, as soon as I suspected it, I thought it better to come and see if you were still here," she replied.

"Really, Claire. You should know better... Everybody knows I practically live here!" he said sarcastically with a grin.

"Okay let's go and have a word with him then." He rose from his desk and marched over to the door, following on behind the nurse down the corridor to Harvey's room.

"How's Max?" he asked enquiring after her boyfriend.

"Oh… Max is Max, he's hoping that we'll be able to buy a house next year." She could hardly wait.

"Well, send him my regards the next time you see him," he replied making small talk.

Harvey Walters was lying flat on his back in bed. *Okay I was shot, I'm a bodyguard. Seems like a short term profession to me,* he thought. *My name is… my name is… Oh, Christ!*

A moment later, Dr Stone entered the room with Nurse Stevens in tow.

"Ah the patient is awake! Well that is a good start. Right, well, Mr Walters…" he began, perching on the side of the bed. "I must inform you that you've been in a terrible incident and your body has been through an ordeal, so some things may seem a bit strange to you for a while".

"Doc…" he paused, feeling his next statement might sound stupid. "I don't remember my name." He winced.

"I see. Well that's not altogether unusual for somebody who has been through such a trauma. But more often than not, patients can be expected to make a full recovery. Just relax as much as you can and let's try and work backwards and hopefully we can find a starting point to work from. What is your first memory?" asked the doctor reassuringly.

Harvey thought back for a moment. "My mother's name is Jessica. I can't think of my Dad's though."

"Okay..." Dr Stone frowned. He continued with his line of questioning for several minutes before announcing, "Well, I think it's safe to assume you've not got full blown amnesia, Harvey, which is good. Tell me, do you remember your wife's name?"

"What? I'm married? Christ, I wonder what she's like. Wait... I think she's called Chloe."

"Well, close. That's your daughter's name," said the doctor, looking at the get well card by the flowers. "I guess you haven't read this yet." He passed Harvey the card.

"Blimey," he mumbled reading the card. "I feel like I've got married and had two kids, all in one evening...!" He looked up at the doctor. "Doesn't it strike you as kind of odd, that her husband is lying in bed having been shot and she's not here?"

The doctor shot a glance at the nurse whose eyes dropped to the floor. He turned to take the clip board off the end of the bed. Staring at the board he sheepishly replied,

"Well I'm sure there is a good reason. After all you've been unconscious. There was not a lot that she could have accomplished here."

"She has called a couple of times though," interrupted the nurse.

"Anyway, it's getting late. You should try to rest and we'll continue on in the morning. I think your boss will be visiting you too."

"What's his name?"

"Inspector Bickley. Don't think on it more tonight though. Simply try and get some rest... goodnight," he said as he turned to leave.

"I'm going off duty now," added Nurse Stevens. "But if you need anything during the night, press that button and Nurse Hawkins will come and see you," she said tucking his sheets making sure he was comfortable. "Goodnight." she added with the weary smile of someone attempting badly to hide the fact she was clearly overworked.

"Thank you, goodnight," he responded.

Harvey lay in his private room and looked around at his sparse surroundings. There was a hand basin and mirror in the corner, and a television suspended from the ceiling. But, apart from that, it was just a typical hospital room. The bed with a mechanism to allow its resident to sit in a number of different reclining positions and a couple of panic buttons to call the staff. He had a table upon which was a hospital vase with flowers from his family, lovingly arranged by the nurse who had become accustomed to the task. There were bags dangling by his bed pumping various different types of medicine via intravenous drip into his arm. He looked for a remote control or some method of turning on the television but couldn't see any, short of getting out of bed and doing it manually. In the end he opted to sleep hoping that he might dream and recall some of the detail of his recent past.

It was mid-morning the following day by the time Harvey's mother arrived at the Royal Devon & Exeter Hospital.

"Good morning," said Jessica. "I wonder if you could help me. I'm looking for Harvey Walters".

"I'm sorry, madam. He's not allowed visitors at the moment," replied the receptionist.

"I was led to believe he was out of intensive care now. You see, I travelled down from London last night to see him." Jessica began welling up inside for the thought of travelling so far to see her only son and being prohibited by a receptionist.

"I'm sorry, madam. Rules are rules I'm afraid."

"Well that's preposterous. You cannot stop me from seeing my son!" Her voice loud but shaky, she started to look around for some indication of where the wards were situated.

Dr Stone overheard the commotion as he walked back from an Accident and Emergency case. He had barely arrived himself when an injured motorist had been brought in by ambulance. He sauntered over to reception to see if any intervention was required. It was not unusual at this part of the hospital to hear verbal clashes, either due to the queues or relatives visiting at odd hours of the night. Normally a few soft words from someone in authority would calm a situation down.

"Excuse me, madam. My name is Dr Stone. Is there a problem here?" he asked politely.

"They won't let me see my Harvey!" Jessica wailed. She threw her arms around Dr Stone as though he was a lifelong friend and burrowed her forehead into his chest whilst her tears flowed.

"Okay, I'll take care of this," he said to the receptionist. "Alright Mrs... Mrs...?"

"Walters," mouthed the receptionist. "Ah... Walters? We may have something in common, Mrs Walters. I believe I have a Mr Walters as one of my patients," he said, thanking heaven they now had a topic of conversation available of interest to the two of them. "Let's go up to my office and get you a nice hot cup of tea," he chuckled and continued "Well, I say nice, but I think beauty is truly in the eye of the beholder when it comes to tea in the R, D & E." He looked at her. A slight smile appeared on her face.

Arriving at his office a couple of minutes later, he offered her a seat and took up his place behind the desk. He looked across at her and suddenly felt quite awkward. He hadn't really seen her face before, but realised he had just taken her from one side of the hospital to the other without offering her as much as a tissue. She was a sight. Mascara had flowed all down her face, not to mention on his white coat come to that, he thought looking down his front. This would not do. A respite was required to allow her to regain her composure.

"Mrs Walters," he started, taking a box of tissues from his desk drawer and sliding them across his desk to her. "I shall go and find you a cup of tea. I imagine it will take at least five minutes or so. The canteen is always so busy. Feel free whilst I'm away to use the mirror in the corner to err…" His mind went blank "to err…" he rose and became agitated. It was not often he got caught lost for words. He rolled his hands as though thinking on an appropriate comment but had almost conveniently stuttered his way out of his office before having a chance to think of something apt to say.

She realised immediately what was occurring and nodded her head. She braved a chuckle like a nervous and embarrassed school girl and wiped at her eyes while continuing to sniff profusely. Dr Stone left his office and went in search of a cup of tea.

Jessica re-embarked on her wailing for a few moments after he had left the office before once again regaining her composure. She took a moment before standing up and crossing the room to the sink.

Dr Stone's office was little more than a converted private patient's room; the desk simply replacing the bed. He had put various medical posters and year planners up on the wall to make it more like an office and Jessica noticed a picture of him, presumably with his wife and daughter at the girl's university graduation, propped neatly on his desk. It was not difficult to see that this busy little office was probably a product of budget cuts, and moreover bed closures, within the hospital.

Jessica looked at herself in the mirror, her eyes all puffy with traces of mascara trailing down her cheeks. Her eyes had taken the double hit of shattered emotion and physical fatigue from the long journey down from London the night before. She hadn't slept much even in the luxurious surroundings of The Forte Crest hotel at Southernhay, in Exeter city centre.

She hurriedly got to work on repairing her face; she was a proud lady and felt slightly wounded that the doctor had seen her in such a state. Dr Stone meanwhile, had decided to leave it ten minutes to ensure he did not disturb Mrs Walters mid-stream. He thought looking at a lady before she was happy with her make-up was as bad as walking in on her half-dressed, and with her current disposition, he had no wish to further her embarrassment.

A short while later he gently nudged the door open trying not to spill either of the cups of tea. He cautiously manoeuvred across to the desk to put them down.

"Here we are," he said, a self-gratifying smile strewn across his face for not spilling a drop.

He sat down at his desk and finally saw Mrs Walters for what she was; a rather stunning lady for her age, although her eyes were still slightly puffy from her tears. He could see past that and decided she was very pleasing to the eye. "Have you travelled far, Mrs Walters?" he enquired.

"Please, it's Jessica. I travelled from London last night. I'm staying at the Forte Crest in Southernhay. How is Harvey?" she implored.

"Well, Jessica. I understand your concern. I have a daughter of my own," he replied proudly pointing to the picture of his daughter. "Your son is a very lucky man. He is stable now but, there have been some repercussions following his ordeal."

"Oh!" she gasped, covering her mouth with her hands.

"We think it's temporary but, he is suffering from amnesia. We haven't let him have visitors until today as we don't want to increase his anxiety. In fact, today could be a busy day for him. His boss is hoping to speak to him as well."

"Who Greg? Greg is here?" she asked.

"That's right. Inspector Bickley. But unfortunately Harvey doesn't recognise him. He does however remember you, in name at least. So, it is just as well you are here to break the ice, so to speak."

"He's an only child you know. I've been so worried," she announced, clenching her hands on top of her lap.

"Well, I assure you, as one parent to another, the worst is over. May I ask; is there a Mr Walters?" asked Dr Stone recalling Harvey's lack of knowledge for his father's name.

"I'm afraid he passed away when Harvey was a toddler."

"How dreadful for you," replied the doctor. "I've been alone myself for a number of years. It's terrible when families break up whatever the reason."

"Yes we've been through some difficult times." Her mind wandered aimlessly through distant memories of name calling and the pity she received from her peers.

It had been far from fashionable to be a single mother back then.

"Are you planning to stay throughout Harvey's convalescence?"

"I plan to stay for as long as he needs me."

"Marvellous. That should speed things up nicely. Well, I think we should go along and reunite the two of you," said the doctor, once again standing up confidently from his chair. He beckoned Jessica towards the door. "After you," he gestured with a smile.

"Thank you, doctor," she responded.

"Harvey... Oh Harvey..." Jessica exclaimed as she saw him for the first time. "What have you been up to?" she continued, scorning him as though he was a naughty child.

"Mother, for goodness sake. I've been shot. I've not just been in some brawl!" he wanted to reply, but the words failed to reach his mouth and he lay in silence like a chastised school boy.

"Oh, Harvey. Thank goodness you are okay," she continued, lunging over the bed to cradle him.

Dr Stone looked at nurse Stevens who had been tending to him and they exchanged smirks.

"Well, Harvey. I guess we can assume that you can remember your mother alright?" said Dr Stone, holding back from chuckling at Harvey's over protective mother.

Harvey simply nodded and raising his eyebrows painfully forced a smirk towards his mother.

"Okay. Well, I think we'll take our leave. I'm sure that the two of you have got a lot to talk about," said the doctor, ushering nurse Stevens out of the room.
"Thank you, doctor," said Jessica gazing up at him.

"If you need anything I'll be in my office," he said smiling back at her.

Without so much as a pause after the door closed behind Dr Stone, Jessica inappropriately put on her mothering hat.

"Goodness gracious, Harvey. I told you not to get involved in that... that body guarding nonsense! What kind of a job is that anyway? Throwing yourself in front of bullets intended for someone else, for goodness sake!" Her feelings raging as though she'd forgotten he'd been injured at all.

"Mother calm down. I'm okay." The words this time reached his mouth, escaping with a raspy inflection. "I wasn't the target, the guy was just a lousy shot!" he said, exasperated yet trying to force a grin.

Jessica sat up, looked him in the eye and amended her tone. "Oh, Harvey. I just don't know what I'd do if anything happened to you," she said, frowning as a tear reappeared trickling down the side of her cheek. She leant over and embraced him once again.

"How are you mother?" said Harvey trying to break the somewhat morbid line of conversation.

"Oh, I'm okay..."

Harvey looked around and pointed towards a jug of water on the side table. Jessica instinctively responded, assisting him in taking on board some much needed liquids. The water slipped down his throat effortlessly and Harvey sighed with relief.

"Mother, I don't recall any memories of my father. What is his name?" he innocently asked, his voice still strained but slowly returning to a more ordinary tone.

The question hit Jessica like a thunderbolt out of a clear blue sky.

"His name was Christian, dear. He died when you were a toddler," she said tentatively.

"Oh," he said, saddened and glancing away. "I guess that'll explain why I don't remember him. Do you have any pictures of him?" he continued, refusing to let the subject pass.

Jessica's persona changed. She had always managed to steer him away from the subject before. He had seen pictures of him around the house but they were like bits of furniture and had largely gone unnoticed.

"I'm sure I could dig one out. Why the sudden interest Harvey?"

Harvey noted a sinister tone in her voice.

"Mother, I've just lost my memory. I need to rebuild my past!" replied Harvey with contempt. "Did you not get on?" he enquired, determined to get to the bottom of this mood change.

"On the contrary, we had many years of happiness together. I just wish he was here to share you with me."

This seemed to satisfy Harvey for the time being, and the subject appeared to be closed.

Greg Bickley stood at reception as the tannoy went out for Dr Stone. He had encountered similar problems as Jessica earlier in the day. Dr Stone approached holding out his hand in greeting.

"Inspector Bickley, good morning," he said shaking him by the hand.

"I see security has been stepped up around Harvey?"

"No, just over enthusiastic staff I'm afraid," replied the doctor with a wink to the receptionist.

"Well, doc. Can I see him today?"

"Yes, but we must tread carefully as he appears not to remember you."

"Oh, brother. That's all we need. How did that happen?"

"It's quite common when a person goes through life threatening situations like this. The mind blots bad memories out. Does he have any bad memories of you?"

"Well, let us just say we've had our moments together," replied Greg, thinking back to what seemed like another world.

Greg and Harvey hadn't spent their whole careers together, but had become soul mates after the Bournemouth murders in 1982. Harvey had spent some time working for the Criminal Investigations Department, a prized job for a policeman as there were extra pay benefits. He then moved on to the Drug Squad during the summer of 1987.

At twenty six, Harvey felt he had seen more than his fair share of nasty events. His once thick black hair was already beginning to grey. His medium build had not changed externally, although through years of training he had developed a six pack and what was once puppy fat had been converted into solid muscle. Like many others in the drug squad, he had to learn to be inconspicuous, which inevitably meant letting his appearance go, so as to fit in with the low lives that he would be forced to become acquainted with. He had developed a goatee beard which he had grown fond of. It had converted his facial appearance from being a healthy, handsome young man into a somewhat mean looking tyrant. He was exactly what the department had been looking for.

"Harvey," called the superintendent. "I need to see you in my office right away."

"What can I do for you sir?" he asked on entering the office.

"Come in and shut the door, Harvey. You know Greg Bickley I take it?" Greg was sat down by the desk.

"Yes, sir. Hi, Greg," he said holding out his hand. The situation did not seem appropriate for their usual greeting as good friends.

"Greg's heading a team in cooperation with the Americans. I want to put an officer in deep cover within the Giordano mob. If you accept this assignment, you'll need to get your house in order before you go as you could be gone some time." He stared into Harvey's eyes. "It is a volunteer assignment, Harvey. Do you think you're ready for it?"

"Yeah, how long before we go?" asked Harvey his heart going crazy at the thought of this opportunity.

"One week. You leave next Tuesday. Greg can give you the details." The superintendent felt guilty. He didn't like sending married personnel on operations such as this, especially overseas. "Okay that is all. Oh, Harv… good luck!" he added.

Greg and Harvey got up and left the office quietly. Once outside, Greg put his arm over Harvey's shoulder. "How the hell are you doing, Harv?" he said boisterously.

"Top drawer, and you?" he said grinning wildly.

"Banging people behind bars as usual!" he replied.

"How's Jenny going to take to this new assignment?" Harvey stopped dead in his tracks, having been overwhelmed by this opportunity. "Oh Christ… I never thought."

"Oh dear," he muttered in caution. "Looks like roses could be called for. You do realise there'll be no contact… could be a couple of years!" he added, exaggerating wildly.

"Thanks for making me feel better, Greg," said Harvey anxiously. "If I make it past Jenny alive, the mob should be a breeze!"

The next week passed painfully slowly. Jenny hadn't taken well to the idea of Harvey going away on a non-contact detachment. He had encouraged her to speak to other wives who had gone through similar experiences, but underestimated how candid they would be.

"They never think of the people they leave behind. You sit day after day not knowing whether they're dead or alive, occasionally getting a visit from someone in the department with little or no news. Each time they knock on the door wondering whether today will be the day you become a widow... never again," said one.

"Assume he's not coming back and get on with your life," advised another.

This hadn't been at all the support that Harvey had in mind. It made the week a bitter challenge.

Tuesday eventually came around and Greg had arranged to collect Harvey from home. Jenny already held Greg largely to blame for this assignment and on his arrival, avoided any eye contact with him.

"Darling, I'll be thinking of you every minute, please hang on in there. Don't give up on me." A lump developing in his throat as he picked up Chloe and Rob, one in each arm, and squeezed them tight wondering how he would bear being apart from them for so long.

"I'm afraid we have to go now Jenny," said Greg equally unable to make eye contact. She managed to cast him an icy stare, and turning to go he continued in a defeated manner, "Harvey, I'll wait in the car."

Jenny grabbed Harvey with both arms. "You just… just take care and let me know how you are if you can," she said tearfully, trying to maintain a brave face.

Harvey gave her one last kiss and walked to the car. He didn't look back. He couldn't bear to. Jenny was weeping furiously and his own eyes began to swell.

Greg and Harvey would travel on to hitch a lift from RAF Brize Norton. There was a Royal Air Force VC10 Tanker going out on exercise to Nevada. They would be met and briefed by FBI agents before beginning the task of infiltration. It would be a long and arduous task…

8 – Entrance to the Underworld

It was the fourth of August 1982; one week away from what would have been Jack's parents' twenty-fifth wedding anniversary. Jack's visit to their graveside would be missed this year. He had made an effort on their birthdays, anniversaries and at Christmas to lay down flowers and take a moment to recall fond memories of them. It would be some time before he had another opportunity.

The weather was warm and humid at Heathrow's terminal three.

"May I see your passport, please, sir?" asked the attendant.

Jack gave her his passport and first class tickets for Chicago O'Hare International.

"Did you pack the bag yourself?" she said running through the routine list of questions.

"Yes," he replied.

A cold stare his only return.

"You'll be boarding at gate fourteen, sir."

"Thanks," Jack said, retrieving his passport and boarding pass. On making his way towards customs he noticed that the policemen were armed, an unusual sight in the United Kingdom. *No doubt a threat of a bombing from the IRA,* he thought. He proceeded through the metal detectors to the departure gates and headed directly for the bar.

"Cappuccino, please," he politely asked the waitress.

"Would you like anything else, sir?" she enquired.

"No, that's it, thanks." He paid for the drink and headed for a free table. From his table he began watching the business travellers passing by hurriedly, whilst the many families travelling for pleasure, were lured in to the duty free shops to purchase cut price products and books to read on their forthcoming holidays.

– Flight British Airways 248 is now boarding at gate fourteen – bellowed the tannoy.

Jack got up and looked around for signs for gate fourteen. He calmly strolled down the long walkways and on arrival at the gate, he presented his boarding pass to the smartly dressed attendant.

"You'll be at the front of the plane, sir," she informed him. "You'll be boarding first," she continued with which another call came over the tannoy.

– Would any remaining passengers for British Airways flight 248 traveling to Chicago please make their way to boarding gate fourteen immediately –

Jack climbed the stairs to board the plane and once aboard, immediately noticed the first time fliers amongst the passengers nervously reading the safety instructions and scanning around for signs of emergency exits. Others were busily filling the overhead lockers with hand luggage and duty free. He glanced to his right to see a smart businessman already settled and looking through his papers, no doubt on his way to Chicago to make his latest deal, craving the commission that would feed his family for the next year or so. Jack wondered how it would feel to be normal. Their eyes met.

"Hi. Rick Kane," the man said, offering his name.

"Jack Shaw, have you flown before?" Jack responded politely.

"Sure, about once a month. I hear it's going to be rough tonight!"

"Well, we'll just have to roll with the punches!" he replied, taking his seat.

"I guess so."

Jack wasn't a frequent flyer and recalled a rather hair raising flight as a youngster with his parents travelling on holiday to Barcelona. He didn't relish the idea of a harsh long haul experience. He settled himself into the seat before glancing up to see the flight attendants marching up and down the aisle, their false smiles firmly attached, assisting the final passengers in finding their seats.

"Could you fasten your seat belt please, sir?" asked the passing attendant, as she checked every row for those non-compliant passengers ignoring the illuminated signs.

She passed Jack, her permanent smile attempting to put Jack at ease. He had wondered how such people managed to maintain it for such long periods of time and, considered how different their inner thoughts might be to their outward appearance.

Within minutes, all of the passengers were settled and the captain switched on the tannoy system announcing their imminent take off.

Moments later the G-force could be felt as the beast of a plane attempted to become airborne. The jet engines straining to get up to speed before finally lifting the wheels off the tarmac. Jack called for the attendant as the plane rose to some 33,000 feet.

"Excuse me, can I get a drink?"

"What would you like, sir?" she responded.

"Vodka on the rocks," he replied. "Do you want one Rick?"

"No, I'm okay, thanks," replied Rick, clearly engrossed in some editorial of the in-flight magazine.

"That will be all, thanks," he said whilst staring into her hazel brown eyes.

To Jack's delight, the entire flight passed almost without incident. There was some turbulence on the way, but nothing too out of the ordinary. When they finally landed, some several hours later, the tannoy came to life once again;

– Please remain seated until we are stationary at the International terminal building – instructed the

voice of the stewardess, with which several people immediately got out of their seats and started unloading the overhead lockers.

Having consumed his vodka and exchanged pleasantries with Rick, he had quickly settled back in his seat and drifted off to sleep. He'd had a bad experience with in-flight food previously and first class or not, he had decided not to wait up for the meal.

The flight had passed incredibly quickly for him. He had slept straight through it and dreamt about home. He'd spent most of the previous week covering furniture with dust sheets and locking away his most valuable items in the house. He had taken on a security box at a local bank for his mother's jewellery, which had lain almost untouched where she had left it that fateful night over two years before. He hoped that one day, he would find someone worthy enough to display it in all its glory once again.

Lucio had assured him that they would keep a close eye on the house and Jack volunteered him the keys to let cleaners in once in a while. He was expecting to be away for some time. Before leaving, Jack had sent a message to Lee as he'd been unable to contact her as promised. He wasn't entirely sure why he bothered, perhaps through professional courtesy, to say he would be absent for a while. He wondered if she would do long haul appointments.

Rick broke Jack's train of thought.

"Doesn't it just amaze you?"

"Sorry, what?" replied Jack.

"Please remain in your seats until we're at the terminal… so what do these sheep do? Immediately get out of their seats and start queuing." He chuckled. "Unbelievable!" His voice could be clearly heard by other passengers who looked resentful at his comments, but all the same, knew he was correct.

"Are you being met at the terminal?" asked Jack.

"No. I'll be hiring a car and making my own way to the hotel, and you?"

"I'm expecting to be picked up by friends," replied Jack, wondering what these friends might look like, or how they would even contact him. Lucio had been deliberately uninformative about his relatives. "Don't worry. You'll know them when you see them, Jack," he had said.

Jack looked out of the window to see the ground crew running around, fixing the chocks under the wheels and preparing for the refuelling process. He could see the luggage already being removed from the holds and then, as the doors were opened to allow the passengers to exit, he felt the rush of warm air enter the aircraft. He waited patiently in his seat as the queue thinned and then calmly got up. As he stretched, he heard his stomach rumble impatiently. It had been almost ten hours since his last meal. He would get a take away in the terminal.

Following the crowd through the tunnel and towards baggage reclaim; it struck him that the size of the airport made its UK counterparts appear very insignificant. The passengers all huddled together at baggage reclaim for twenty minutes or so before the first of the flight's baggage began to appear on the revolving conveyor. Eventually, Jack caught sight of his own large suitcase and walked to the conveyor to lift it.

He launched it on to a trolley and felt a hand on his shoulder. Turning, half expecting to see his travelling mate Rick, he was taken aback.
"Jack, is that you?" came the friendly voice from a man he'd never seen before in his life.

In his confusion Jack nodded. "Err....yes."

"Jack, my friend. It's been years. It's so great to see you." He added in a whisper, "Act like we're buddies. I'm Lucio's cousin Vinny and we're on camera."

"Vinny! How have you been?" Jack exclaimed, feeling quite uneasy about entering such a charade with a complete stranger. He played along hoping the reason would soon become clear. Vinny helped Jack with his case and steered him towards a side exit where a security guard swiftly opened the door to let them through. To Jack's surprise, it was not only Vinny who entered with him, but four other stern faced men following on behind them. Vinny passed the guard when Jack noticed him crossing the security guard's palm with what looked like, a one hundred dollar bill.

"Why not just wait at the other side of customs for me?" asked Jack. He received no reply.

Vinny motioned to his four counterparts. Two ran ahead and two remained keeping a watchful eye behind them. Jack was unnerved by this whole dramatic scene and was relieved when they finally, after several minutes of walking through empty corridors, reached the open air and to their car. Having taken the scenic route around the airport after leaving baggage reclaim, they hadn't encountered a single airport official.

"I'm sorry about that, Jack. We've been experiencing a few problems recently," Vinny eventually said. "More than likely, if you'd gone the customs route, you would have come out in a pine box."

"Oh, I see," Jack responded nervously.

"We'll be taking you to Don Giordano's place tonight. You'll be safe there. He's keen to meet you after the Bournemouth job."

"News travels fast," said Jack, wondering what exactly Lucio had told them.

"Only in the right circles!" spouted Vinny, who then spent most of the half hour journey speaking in Italian to the driver.

They drew near to the Giordano estate and Jack looked out of the window. He saw two large granite pillars signifying the entrance, each mounted with antique sculptures of African lions. There was a large iron gate between them to keep out unwanted visitors.

Jack watched as the gates retreated slowly to allow the cars through. He noticed the modern surveillance cameras strategically placed all around them and wondered how anyone could tolerate living with, what appeared on the outside to be, such fear. They slowly passed through the gates and Jack observed two suited individuals bearing automatic weapons across their shoulders. He turned to Vinny.

"Can I assume the Don is not too popular?" he asked, in awe of the massive security.

"Everybody has enemies, Jack," he replied. "Welcome to America."

Jack sat back in his seat. He had imagined Lucio to be as big a gangster as he would come across. It appeared that, perhaps he just held a franchise in this business. They pulled up in front of the main house; a magnificent building fit for royalty. Vinny got out of the car first and stepped back to open Jack's door.

"It's okay, I've got it!" yelled Jack impressed at meeting a mobster with manners.

"Okay, Jack. Let's introduce you to the Don. A word of warning. He doesn't like jokes from strangers. And don't reach into your pockets without warning."

"Why is that?" asked Jack naively.

"You'll hit the floor before you have a chance to take your hand out again," he replied sternly.

Jack felt an uncomfortable chill race through his body, the sincerity in Vinny's voice hitting home.

"I'll be careful not to do that then," he muttered under his breath.

Out of the corner of his eye, Jack's attention became drawn to something moving quickly in the distance. He glanced across to the pasture on his right and observed a magnificent white stallion, straddled by a twenty something young lady. Turning back to Vinny he asked, "Who is that?"

The young lady cast a wave to Vinny and he waved back.

"That is the Don's daughter, Natasha. And you'd do well to stay away," he added, seeing the mischievous look in Jack's eye.

Jack was quickly becoming unnerved by the straight speaking and somewhat hostile nature of his host. But before he could say anything further, they reached the entrance of the house and, were greeted by an old man at the front door who managed to put him more at ease.

"Ah, Mr Vincent. The Don is expecting you in the drawing room."

"Thanks, Henry. We'll make our own way there." He looked at Jack as they walked through the palatial hall and whispered "He's the only other English guy here. Used to work for a Duke or something but got caught pinching stuff and was fired."

"…and you trust him?" asked Jack in a surprised tone.

"Never heard of honour among thieves, Jack?"

"Yeah but I was led to believe recently, that it doesn't work too well in practice," he said thinking of Swifty.

"He's been with us over ten years now. He's trustworthy enough."

Arriving at a door, some ten foot high, Vinny knocked loudly using his fist to knock the timber.

Without hearing a response he then opened it and looked around before continuing in and beckoning Jack to follow. Jack scurried behind like a puppy on a lead, not relishing the thought of getting lost as a stranger in an environment with more armed guards than a high security prison.

Beside the huge stone fireplace sat a man mature in years. He appeared to be in deep thought, staring forward but at nothing specific, almost unaware of their presence. Above the fireplace hung a large oil painting, which bore an uncanny resemblance to the man, although perhaps in another era. Jack guessed it must have been his father or grandfather. They approached the man who turned his head to look at Jack. Jack felt instantly intimidated by him. It was almost as if he was immortal, a look from a man who had almost too much knowledge to bear, that nothing could possibly surprise him.

"Don Giordano. May I introduce Jack Shaw?" said Vinny.

"Thank you, Vincent. Leave us," he said dismissing Vinny like a common servant. Vinny looked at Jack clearly upset at being treated this way in front of a stranger. Nevertheless, he was compliant. Turning without another spoken word, he left the room. This intrigued Jack greatly. He wondered what kind of a self-respecting mobster would react so sheepishly.

"He is a good boy but still has a lot to learn," said the Don turning his attention to Jack.

"Don Giordano, may I say how honoured I am to meet you," said Jack trying to muster a friendly smile.

"I have brought a gift for you, but my suitcase seems to have been taken care of for me."

The Don reached for the phone. "Bring Jack's bag to me." He did not mince his words and replaced the phone.

Moments later the door opened and Henry walked in bearing the bag. Jack turned to see Henry, he noticed in the corner of his eye more security cameras watching him. Henry handed the bag to Jack who paused for a moment recalling Vinny's words clearly. He turned to the Don;

"May I?" he asked warily.

"You seem like a sensible gentleman," replied the Don as his eyes were still sizing up Jack. "Go ahead."

"I purchased this on my last visit to London," he said, reaching into the bag. He would have said anything to remain in dialogue with the Don, not wishing for any suspicions to arise or create an incident. He slowly pulled out a bag marked 'Harrods' and although the present was wrapped, he chose to pass it to the Don, erring on the side of caution once more.

The Don looked at Jack. His curiosity and respect for the young man growing with every moment.

"You should become a politician, Jack," he said, referring to the way he was handling this unfamiliar situation.

Jack smiled but said nothing, hoping that the Don would still be so complimentary after seeing his gift. The Don reached into the bag taking out the cube shaped box gift wrapped in Harrods unique style. He looked at Jack curiously, gradually wearing a smile.

"Ah... a watch," he guessed. "Thank you, Jack."

Jack seemingly dumbfounded, his jaw dropped.

"How do you know?" he asked alarmingly.

"Jack," said the Don "you don't live to be my age in this business without a little intuition!" He smirked as he held the gift and began slowly removing the outer wrapping whilst staring at Jack dead in the eye. Uncovering a box, he lifted the lid and momentarily allowed his eyes to relinquish their grip on Jack to observe the gift. On seeing the contents, the Don immediately snapped the lid closed again, his smirk replaced with the look of a predator about to devour its prey. Time stood still for a moment. Jack was left unsure what to say and nervously broke the silence.

"I hope you like it, Don."

The Don's gaze transfixed back on Jack momentarily, he lifted open the lid once again, looked at Jack and laughed out aloud.

"Lucio said you were a slippery character, Jack." He marched over to Jack, embraced him and kissed him on both cheeks. "Welcome to America, my friend." Jack's relief clearly visible he replied

"I am glad to have pleased you, Don."

The Don looked once more into the box admiring the exquisitely designed Faberge Egg once owned by the Romanov's of Russia. Lucio had encouraged this vastly expensive present assuring Jack that in investment terms it would be unrivalled.

"I feel outwitted, Jack. For the first time in a long while. Lucio was correct. You could become a great asset to my organisation."

Jack finally felt the pressure of the meeting ease slightly. In tandem the tension eased from within his body.

"Jack, I have a long standing employee." He stopped to consider how to continue. "Whom I feel should retire, but I need someone to take over his position. I have had feelers out for well over a year now but..." He paused. Gesturing with his hands he continued, "... nothing. Then out of the blue Lucio gave me a call and told me about you." He stopped to gauge Jack's body language, Jack looking unfazed he continued. "Lucio told me about your time in prison and your loyalty in carrying out the Bournemouth job, but..." He took another breath considering each word before he spoke. "He was concerned about your motivation whilst carrying out the job. You are a raw talent Jack, but if you are to work for me, it is imperative that you adopt our precise ways of working. It is better for all involved." He awaited Jack's response.

"There were other considerations in Bournemouth, Don Giordano. But I assure you that I am a quick learner," he replied in an attempt to defend his seemingly psychotic and adrenaline fuelled actions.

"Jack... When working for me, there is only one consideration and that is... working for me! You will carry out the job in whichever way I specify. Do we understand each other?"

Jack's mind was racing ahead wondering what would come next. He bowed down to the Don remembering the disputes he used to have with his father, reminiscing how his father had always been right.

"I understand perfectly Don Giordano."

"Jack... This man I'm retiring is well respected. In fact, some say he's my right hand man. I want him to teach you all he knows and perhaps one day you may take his place, not just his job," he said, dangling a carrot of unknown quantity.

Jack was stunned and didn't know how to respond. *Right hand man to the Don?* he thought.

"Shit, that's ridiculous, why me?"

"Why you?" enquired the Don, Jack being unaware that his final thought had reached his mouth. "For a start, what type of hit man offers a potential boss a gift of more than he could earn in a year? Jack, you have class and, from what I gather, you're not stupid. I need someone of new blood like you to shake up my organisation." He paused. "I'm not saying it won't be dangerous for you Jack, because it will... I am aware that many of my relatives are already queuing to take my place and, they will resent an insertion into the family. But on the other hand, you are young, respectable... you could create solid contacts within the establishment for us."

Jack sat and considered his future. The Don was right about the Faberge Egg. It had cost him close to £250,000.00 quite a dent in his own small fortune, but Lucio had been adamant that it would be worth his while, and he was beginning to understand how.

"What are your terms?" asked Jack.

"I'll pay you $250,000.00 a year retainer, and once you start actively working for me, there will be considerable bonuses," said the poker faced Don.

Jack hardly knew how to react. Legal or not, this was an offer hard to refuse.

"But Don, with respect. You don't know me. What makes you think I'm worth that sort of money?"

"Let's just call it a hunch, eh?" he replied. "If you're in agreement, you will start tomorrow."

Jack stared into the Don's eyes searching for the con man element about him. But he couldn't find it due to the years of experience that the Don possessed.

"Don Giordano, it would be an honour." A smile appeared on Jack's face and the conversion had been completed.

Within a few short hours of reaching US soil Jack Shaw had entered the underworld.

9 – The Detachment

The trip to Brize Norton was slow, Harvey's mind preoccupied with thoughts of his family. The thought of a prolonged absence from his Jenny and the children was already playing on his mind. He wondered how she would cope with Chloe and Rob on her own during their separation. Already he was feeling remorseful for accepting the assignment.

"Are you with us?" asked Greg sensing his mood. "She blames me, doesn't she?" he continued.

"No, of course not, Greg," Harvey responded, in an attempt to lie, wishing to make his friend feel better.

"Well, I guess I'm going to have to keep a close eye on you if she's ever going to talk to me again," he laughed.

"Greg, what's my cover for this gig anyway?" asked Harvey, wishing to steer the conversation away from family matters.

"Well, we were going to wait for the FBI guys to brief you. I hear they've invented you as a fairly nasty criminal called Bill Moore," he replied. "During the last month or so, they've carried out a few high profile robberies for which you, Mr Moore, are responsible."

Harvey wondered what it would be like to live as a criminal. He would need to learn fast if he hoped to survive the detachment.

"Am I high or low profile?" he asked referring to his expected demeanour as a criminal.

"Well, I believe you're high profile right now but rough around the edges. You're best keeping your questions for the Americans, Harv. After all, it is their party."

Harvey sat back impatiently, his mind trying to prematurely explore how he might best conceive this criminal lifestyle.

Greg pointed ahead of them. "There it is, we are almost there," he said.

Harvey looked ahead and could see a military plane the size of a passenger jet circling above.

"I wonder what's stopping them from landing," he said, looking up at the VC10 which was conducting training runs around the airfield.

"Who knows? Judging by its size it may be our ride," replied Greg naively.

Within a few minutes they arrived at the camp gates and pulled up at the guardroom to ask directions. Greg left Harvey waiting in the car while he entered to collect their prearranged passes. It was only a few minutes before he returned to Harvey's side of the vehicle. Harvey wound down the window.

"What's wrong?" he asked. Greg leant towards the window and replied,

"Have you got your ID on you? Can't get us in without it!"

Harvey stretched for his back pocket, struggling against the seat belt as he manoeuvred to reach his wallet. Greg sensed his difficulties and said sarcastically, "You might try taking the belt off first."

"Okay, wise guy," he laughed, looking at Greg.

Harvey unfastened the seatbelt and went for his wallet again. This time he retrieved it with ease, passing it over to Greg who was beaming from ear to ear. "There you go, now bugger off and make yourself useful," he said cheerfully.

Minutes later Greg returned with temporary station passes for the two of them.

"Right, Harv. The guard says somebody will meet us at 101 Squadron Ops," he said as he climbed back into the car. Looking at his watch he added, "We fly out in three hours so we've got a bit of time to kill."

"Let's head straight up there anyway. I quite fancy having a look around. Have always wondered what they hide behind all this barbed wire," he said referring to the high perimeter fencing that circumnavigated the base.

"Are you serious?" asked Greg amazed as he pulled away from the guardroom. He recognised the disappointment in Harvey's demeanour. "Okay, whatever floats your boat, Harv!" he conceded.

"My father saw service in the RAF you know; during the war. It's one of the only things I know about him," Harvey added to his uninterested partner who already had his mind on where they might find a coffee.

"Okay Biggles. Enough already! I said we'll go take a look," sighed Greg. He pulled up alongside the entry barrier, wound down his window and held out the passes. "We're going to 101 squadron."

The corporal said nothing as he scrutinised their documents.

"Follow this road to the end. It's signposted from there, sir," he said, gesturing the way with his hand.

Greg took back the passes and wound up the window. Looking at Harvey, he said, "Well he was a bundle of joy, wasn't he?" Harvey sniggered.

They found the car park relatively easily. As the guard had said, it was well signposted. Greg parked the car and they both made their way over to the 101 squadron building. They entered to find various squadron memorabilia and a huge dark wooden plaque covered with names and pictures of all those current individuals on the station that mattered. There was no sign of any sort of reception, so they ventured through the main corridor ahead of them, in search of someone who could help them.

Harvey couldn't help but look at the pictures that lined the walls of the corridor ahead of him, pictures of the crews that had served over the years, ranging from the most recent all the way back to the 1920's. Harvey stood staring in disbelief half way down the corridor.

"Come on, Harv. Let's get on with it," said Greg, anxious to find someone who could point them in the right direction.

"Jesus, I don't believe it!" gasped Harvey. "Greg take a look at this," he said motioning towards one of the pictures.

Greg shrugged.

"What is it?" he enquired, walking back towards Harvey.

"It's my old man," he said. "I can't believe it!"

Greg looked at the picture. "Wishful thinking my friend. That guy ain't called Walters," said Greg, pointing to the names below the picture.

"Oh!" Harvey sounded confused and embarrassed. "Yeah, I guess you're right. That's uncanny though," he said turning to follow Greg.

Harvey followed Greg down the corridor and Greg turned into another room marked, *101 Sqn Crew room.* Harvey followed on behind.

"Excuse me," called across an ageing officer. From behind an impressive oak bar he continued to help himself to coffee, paused then briefly added. "Can I help you?"

"Ah, yes. We were pointed in this direction. We're from the Met… Err." He stuttered, searching for something less informative to say about their presence before continuing. "We're due to hitch a lift to America on a VC10 this afternoon," said Greg.

"Good for you," replied the officer. "Help yourselves to coffee. 'Fraid there's not many of us in yet. Pre-flight brief isn't for another hour." The officer looked them both up and down. "You're not expecting to fly like that I hope!" he laughed, pointing to their suits.

"Well, we don't have anything else," replied Harvey, shrugging his shoulders and looking to Greg for answers.

"Don't worry. We'll get you down to flying clothing and get you kitted out. I'm sorry, damned rude of me," said the officer realising they hadn't been introduced. "I'm Wing Commander Ferrous. I'll be piloting the plane."

"Pleased to meet you. I'm Greg Bickley and this is my colleague, Harvey Walters."

"It'll probably be a quiet trip. Have you heard the latest?"

Greg looked back across to Harvey for some help this time but Harvey simply looked back shrugging his shoulders.

"Er... The latest?" he enquired.

"Yes. The bottom fell out of the market today. I understand it's still tumbling... I dare not listen to the radio... due to retire next year you see," he mumbled pompously while staring into his mug.

It was October 1987, and indeed the city was in turmoil. Harvey did not follow the stock markets. It was a league to which he aspired, but it would take him some years to amass any sort of saving for investment towards his future.

"Oh!" said Greg tentatively, "I wonder how this'll affect my mortgage?"

"Hah!" roared Ferrous, "Doesn't bear thinking about does it? Well I'm afraid it may cause a few straight faces on the flight."

The three of them stood morbidly in silence before Ferrous piped up. "Look, ole chaps, didn't mean to put a dampener on things. Let's get you kitted up," with which he slammed his mug in the sink. "Come on, follow me," he said, asserting himself.

Greg and Harvey, quite overwhelmed by this eccentric character, sheepishly followed behind Ferrous around the squadron building and out towards a hangar, aptly named 'Supply', where they would be provided flying suits to wear during their journey.

They returned about half an hour later. The crew room was now teeming with people all dressed in similar flying suits. They still could be easily identified as visitors due to the sheen of the new suits and the lack of any name or rank tags. Wing Commander Ferrous led them over to a small stocky gentleman. Harvey looked at his name tag which read Flt Lt *Tiny* Roberts 101 Squadron. Harvey looked across at Greg and they exchanged discreet smirks.

"Tiny, these two chaps are hitching a lift with us. Can you make sure they get to the pre-brief please?" He turned to Greg and Harvey. "I'll see you on board.

You'll be in good hands with Tiny," he added and promptly marched off.

They completed the somewhat unfinished introductions and enquired whether there was time for one last coffee.

"Oh sure," replied Tiny.

"What are you fellas up to in America then?"

"I'm sure you'll understand that we can't…"

"No bother. It's usually the same. Need to know and all that!" he interrupted.

Greg and Harvey felt slightly awkward at not being able to share any information regarding their trip with their hosts, although their hosts seemed quite at home with the fact.

"Oh, have you ordered your food for the trip yet?" Tiny enquired.

"Well, yes. But I've got to admit we thought it was a bit of a wind up to be honest," said Harvey.

"No, it usually sounds grander than it appears on the plate but we all have to eat!" he replied.

"Well, I guess so. Are there many passenger seats on the plane?" asked Greg curiously.

"You are the only passengers today so you should be quite comfortable. That is if you can feel comfortable on a flying petrol station," he laughed. "Okay it looks like its briefing time. Follow me."

Greg and Harvey sat through the briefing, where crew members' roles for the flight ahead were outlined, and the two outsiders were introduced. There was a meteorological brief and details of possible aircraft that may call upon them around the country for fuel. A detailed map was projected onto a large video screen, unveiling the route.

Harvey nudged Greg and whispered,

"It looks like we're going the long way around."

"No kidding," replied Greg.

The brief ended on an inspirational note by Wing Commander Ferrous. It appeared to Greg and Harvey that, for the crew, this trip was little more than an excuse for a jolly and the purchase of duty free and other low cost goods.

"We are in the wrong service," said Harvey sarcastically as they walked back down the corridor with the rest of the crew.

They trooped behind the rest of the crew and boarded a bus which took them out to the waiting plane. The crew's loadmaster, responsible for passengers, cargo and indeed refreshments, eventually took them aboard and to their seats.

"Make yourselves comfortable… It's going to get kind of busy and loud around here until take off. I'll show you around once we're airborne."

"Show us around what?" Greg asked Harvey sarcastically. "Looks pretty simple to me. Pilots live through there and drive, we sit back here and sleep. What's to show?"

"Yeah," laughed Harvey. "Let's just remember we're guests aboard here, Greg." He was all too aware that these were some of the last civilised people he would see for some time.

They could hear the engines winding up, and the Loadmaster came back aboard having carried out his list of outside visual checks.

"Looks like we're off, fellas," he said. "Make sure you're buckled up. We take off on full power unlike our civvy counterparts," he laughed taking his own seat.

A few moments later, the hefty VC10 loaded to capacity with jet fuel, staggered across to line up on the runway. There were no other aircrafts queuing and within moments, they felt their transport lunge forward. Greg and Harvey held on to their armrests as this impressive petrol station was launched down the runway before reaching a safe speed to become airborne.

The VC10 glided up through the sky towards its operating altitude and the air loadmaster unfastened his seat belt and started on more checks. In the cockpit, they would all be doing the same in what for them would be one of the most crucial parts of their flight. Harvey and Greg remained seated, not wishing to interfere with the crew.

Greg had watched as Benny, the air loadmaster, kept going to the rear bay. He had not seen what was back there and was becoming curious as to what checks were being performed on such an aircraft.

"Okay, that's the checks finished for now!" exclaimed Benny over the noise of the engines. "We should level off any minute," he added.

The one thing both Greg and Harvey had noticed was the increase in noise and smell from that of an average private airline. On entering the plane, Harvey had pointed out to Benny what appeared to be a fluid leaking in the vicinity of one of the engines. His comments, far from being seen as stupid, appeared much appreciated by the crew.

Benny had just nodded and said, "Don't worry. If it ain't leaking, it ain't working!" Harvey had thought the reply flippant at the time but while he was harnessing himself into his passenger's seat he had noticed Benny pointing the same thing out to a ground technician outside, getting it double checked before the engines were fired up.

"Do you want the tour now?" Benny asked. Greg and Harvey looked at each other shrugged and nodded.

"Why not?" Greg answered for the two of them. It would help the time pass although neither of them were particularly interested.

They climbed out of their seats and followed Benny to the door of the main fuel compartment. They entered feeling the temperature drop substantially. The compartment consisted of a narrow walkway either side of the fuselage with a metallic tank which spanned the entire centreline of the rest of the aircraft. A number of dials attached to it signified pressure, temperature and capacity. The capacity just read full.

"You mean to tell me this thing's full of fuel? How much?" asked Greg nervously?

"Sorry. Need to know!" shouted back Benny, equalling the score.

"Touché" replied Harvey with a smile.

"But don't worry. We won't run out. The wings are full of the stuff too!"

Greg swallowed hard. The thought of surfing the skies in a flying petrol can didn't seem to agree with his anatomy. He took leave to find the lavatory. Harvey looked across at Benny and laughed. "Weak constitution!" he said loudly.

"Hope we don't hit too much turbulence then," replied Benny. "Let's go up front. I'll show you how we operate the refuelling process." And with that, he turned back towards the front.

Benny took Harvey forward to the cockpit and poured out details on how aircraft were coordinated when refuelling took place. He showed him an array of video monitors that assisted the link up process. Harvey was introduced briefly to the members of the flight deck. Tiny and Ferrous chose to wave, the navigator, Graeme looked up and said,

"Hi," before quickly returning to scribbling furiously on his notepad. The engineer was too busy preparing to accept a group of four Tornados to acknowledge the guest.

"This may interest you. If you go back to the tank and look out of the window behind the wing, you'll see them hooking up," shouted Benny.

"Go starboard side, Harvey. There's a rookie trying to join us," interrupted Ferrous. "They always fuck it up first couple of goes and give us a heartache."

Harvey waved a hand to gesture he was off and disappeared down back again. He saw no sign of Greg. He guessed that he must have taken up residency in the toilet. *Probably just as well,* thought Harvey. If what Ferrous said was true, he might be joining Greg shortly.

He looked out of the window to search the skies for the group of Tornados and without warning, they appeared out of nowhere. Harvey gasped at the awesome sight. Their wingtips couldn't have been more than fifteen feet apart.

He instinctively waved at the pilot and whilst instantly feeling foolish, the pilot returned the compliment. They disappeared out of sight for a moment, dropping back to allow the engineer to wind out the refuelling baskets for their thirsty jets. Moments later, they moved back in. There were two jets on each wing, yet only one basket for refuelling.
I wouldn't like to be the guy waiting in the queue, he thought.

The first jet moved up towards the basket, his wingman giving him space to manoeuvre. He swung around trying to connect, but missed. *Oh shit, this must be the rookie,"* Harvey thought.

Benny had explained that the pilot, flying at 20,000 feet and at a speed of 240 knots, had to slot a rod protruding from his cockpit, no more than two fingers in diameter, into a basket containing the supply pipe, whilst countering the effects of crosswinds.

At the same time, he needed to concentrate on not hitting the VC10 or his wingman who was looking out for him. The conclusion to this situation was always a success. It had to be. The result of the pilot bottling out or being unsuccessful would be a doomed aircraft without enough fuel to get home.

Harvey stood in awe looking through the window while for five minutes while the pilot fought for connection, eventually managing it with less than five minutes of flight time left in the tanks. Benny came down the back.

"Pretty impressive huh?" He added, "Didn't do his wingman any favours though. He's reduced his window substantially. But he's an old timer so there shouldn't be any problems. Soon as we've filled the other two we'll be on our way. Then I'll get us some grub, okay?"

Harvey nodded in agreement adding, "Have you seen Greg?"

"He's chosen the easy option. Sleeping like a baby!" He continued, "Make sure he takes some liquids on board when he wakes, okay. Easy to get dehydrated up here."

"Gotcha!" replied Harvey, but first chose to stick around and see out the rest of the refuelling taking place.

Having refuelled the Tornados, they began the main body of the flight. Benny, true to his word, arrived with some tin trays stuffed with roast chicken, potatoes and vegetables covered in lumpy gravy.

"Greg, it's time to eat," said Harvey, nudging his friend back into consciousness waving the tin tray under his nose. Greg looked up and groaned at the realisation that he was still airborne. They both took their respective trays and started to tuck in.

"I managed to wangle some cream doughnuts for afterwards," Benny shouted with a mischievous grin. "I know the caterer quite well."

Harvey smiled back and continued to eat. The crew appeared appreciative of small treats on this long haul flight. It seemed amazing what it did for their morale, and as a result, Benny was a very popular member of the crew.

They finished the food and enjoyed their doughnuts with piping hot coffee before Harvey proclaimed,

"Thanks, Benny. That was better than any in flight meal I've had before." Benny smiled at the appreciation and Harvey concluded, "I'm going to get some sleep. Give me a shout if I can help with anything."

"I'll wake you on our final approach," replied Benny who himself was rummaging around in his bag for a makeshift pillow.

Harvey tried to get comfortable and rested his eyelids. He would always think of home when trying to sleep. This time, putting away the thoughts of being absent, he thought of teaching Rob how to play football and quite quickly drifted off into never-never land.

Greg looked across at the other two snoozing away and decided to do some work whilst there were no interruptions. He reached for his hand luggage and took out a large file marked, The Phoenix, the profile of a hit man who had gone undetected since the seventies. The authorities thought The Phoenix had gone into retirement, but he seemed to have risen again around 1982 during which time a spate of assassinations, all bearing his hallmarks were carried out. The one lead being that there seemed to be a link with the Giordano cartel, the organisation within which Harvey, would become embroiled.

10 – An Inside Job

Last night at 11.30, a hit man known to the FBI as 'The Phoenix' is believed to have struck again. This man or woman... she added, *continues to elude the authorities after what is believed to have been a career, so far spanning some 17 years, making him as notorious as the international terrorist, The Jackal.*

The latest victim was a high profile Chairman of Patriot Industries Jim Garnish, who was believed to have smuggled weapons to the Argentines during the Falklands conflict with the United Kingdom. The CNN reporter was cut off in mid-stream as Jack hit the off button on his television set. He had been lying on the couch in his casino penthouse apartment relaxing with a gin and tonic when the news had come on. This had been an unconventional job carried out for the FBI.

They had sought The Phoenix's services after their evidence against Garnish had been compromised. The FBI had carried out a costly investigation over a period of some six years. On realising the probability that his lawyers would get him off on a technicality, someone high up the chain of command had decided to make a less than conventional example of him to other arms dealers.

They had approached the mafia, supplied the appropriate information and equipment and paid a substantial non traceable bounty. The job passed through a complex network in the underworld before landing on Jack's doorstep. For Jack the job had been a breeze, carried out at long range, it was easy money. His only worry had been whether *he* was a more important catch to the FBI than the target himself.

"They'll never catch him," Stephan called from the kitchen.

"Oh, what makes you so sure?" asked Jack, curious to hear his colleague's view.

"This guy has been topping people for over seventeen years Jack, and never left so much as a sniff of who he is. He's the master of the trade. A God damned legend!" said Stephan.

Jack smirked. Stephan had been a good friend to him since he had landed in America some five years ago. But it had been agreed with the Don from the outset that, besides himself, only three other people would know The Phoenix's identity; Lucio, Don Giordano and his predecessor, Tony.

Jack had taken to his new profession like a duck to water, although in the first year, he still vented his anger on his victims during close kills. This resulted in some quite horrendous crime scenes being found by officers of the law, most of whom were now either in counselling or had become bitter and twisted, turning bad and taking bribes as their disillusionment with law enforcement grew and their principles deteriorated.

Despite this initial lack of panache on Jack's part, this served its purpose for the Don as it made the police weary and easier to corrupt. Nevertheless, he was concerned that Jack's psychotic methodology would eventually lead the authorities to his door and so, weaned him off this form of killing by assigning him to distance kills. He used The Phoenix to tutor him in the arts of the assassin and taking on targets from a safe distance until no distinguishable difference existed between the work of Jack and that of The Phoenix himself.

"Well, let's drink to The Phoenix then," said Jack raising his glass.

"The Phoenix!" responded Stephan in salute. "Long may he reign," he added.

"So Stephan, how is your side of the business going?" asked Jack, changing the subject and referring to the 'legal' side of the business. "The Don has voiced his concerns to me that profits are down in the casinos. Should he be worried, Stephan?"

Stephan was aware that Jack was a killer, and a fearsome one at that. Most members of the cartel had to kill at one time or another to prove their commitment to the Don. But he was not aware of the extent of Jack's merciless streak or indeed his newly incorporated and infamous identity.

"What are you insinuating Jack?" snorted his insulted friend.

Jack stared deep into Stephan's eyes. "I hear you've been spending a lot of time at the track lately. Do you owe money, Stephan?"

"I'm not sure I like where this is going Jack. And no, I don't."

Jack persisted. "Stephan, we've become good friends these past five years. I can lend you money if you need it." His eyes never left Stephan's gaze.

"Jack, if you've brought me here to question me about my side of the business and directing accusations at me, then you can fuck off!" he stated arrogantly. "I have blood links to this family Jack. I don't ponce around like some outsider who thinks he runs the family," he wailed referring to Jack's position within the family. "You don't scare me Jack!" he concluded.

"Come on, Stephan. Calm down. I asked you out here to have dinner with a friend. If you say there's no problem, then there's no problem. I'm just concerned for you that's all," he said with a smile, putting his arm across Stephan's shoulder.

Stephan looked up at him, angry but also anxious. There had been more bravado than truth in not being scared of Jack.

"We'll go and have dinner. They've got a great lobster special on tonight and your uncle wants to join us. He said he hasn't seen you for a while and would like to catch up," he added, referring to the Don.

"Okay," replied Stephan, attempting to regain his composure.

"I'll just get my coat," said Jack as he wandered into the bedroom.

Jack sat down on the side of his bed and pulled out the ticket. He stared at the numbers and sighed with disappointment. Stephan's ticket had been passed to Jack to honour by the bookie, who had received a less than warm response from Stephan when asked to settle up. The sum on the ticket was over $100,000.00. Jack had a decision to make.

This was not a one off debt. It was simply that Stephan had siphoned so much off the casino's bottom line, that he feared taking any more. The ticket just scratched the surface of how much family money Stephan had gambled away. The question Jack was wrestling with was, whether he would save his friend and put himself in jeopardy or come clean with the Don about his friend's predicament.

Both Jack and the Don had been concerned that embezzlement was taking place within the casinos and hotels in the region. Stephan might be a blood relation to the Don but, should it come to down to it, he wouldn't be the first hit the Don had ordered on his own family, and probably not the last. Jack's concern was that Stephan had been his friend and on more than one occasion had watched his back from other scheming members of the family.

"What's keeping you?" Stephan called from the kitchen.

Jack did not respond but rose from the bed and walked back out to join Stephan. He could not ponder this any longer.

"I thought you were getting your coat?" asked Stephan.

Jack placed the slip of paper on the side board of the kitchen in front of Stephan.

"Pour us both a drink," he said sternly, adopting a father-child stance.

The blood drained from Stephan's face as he reached for the decanter. Jack's revolver, which he carried for day to day protection, was holstered under his jacket, loaded and cocked, just in case.

"We have a choice. You come clean and I help you, or I pass this to the Don at drinks tonight and you take your chances. Which will it be, Stephan?" he asked poker faced, watching every tiny movement of Stephan's body for an indication of a frightened man's reaction to this awesome blow.

Stephan turned slowly to look at Jack. His eyes had grown swollen in those few seconds, as though already resigned to his fate. His typically Italian bravado no longer apparent, his face bore the appearance of a lost child who didn't know where to turn.

"Two million dollars," he murmured with the downbeat tone of a condemned man.

Jack slammed the counter with his fist.

"God Damn it!" he roared. "How the fuck can I protect you against that? You are supposed to be the honest one!" he continued.

Jack paused for a moment's thought, wondering whether there was any way out for his friend. "Jesus. Who is your greatest enemy in the organisation?"

"What?"

"Just answer the fucking question. Who is most likely to screw you over?" asked Jack, clearly maddened following the revelation and full extent of his friend's debt.

"I don't know... err. Lisa Forbes would screw me over for a dime I guess."

"Could she get access to the finances?"

"Of course. She does the accounts. She's always insinuating that she knows everything, always looking for some way to get more authority."

"Perfect. Is this Lisa close to any other family members?" asked Jack.

"No, I don't think so," he replied. "Why? What's this about?"

"Go and have dinner solo, and put it on my tab. Meet with the Don in the bar at 10:00 p.m. if I'm not back. If he asks where I am, tell him our little problem is being taken care of... okay?"

"Okay... What are you going to do?"

"Save your fucking life that's what. We'll talk my terms later, okay?" replied Jack.

"Okay, Jack... Okay."

Jack picked up his coat and left Stephan standing in his apartment while he headed for his office.

Jack had acquired the penthouse apartment above the *Lucky Seven Casino* six months after arriving in

America, much to the disgust of many of the Don's relatives. All were curious why this outsider had been so readily accepted into the family by the Don. They soon realised that Jack was someone to be on the good side of if their relationship with the Don was going to continue in a good light. A couple of ambitious individuals had attempted to go behind the Don and have Jack killed, but this had been expected and only confirmed the Don's suspicions of where their loyalties lay, and where personal ambitions had overridden their loyalty to the Don. They were spared no mercy.

The penthouse had previously belonged to Tony Aka, The Phoenix. He had taken Jack into his world gladly. His wish to retire to the country was granted and he settled down for the first time in his life to as normal an existence as could have been expected. He was one of very few who would actually stay alive to see retirement, most being unable to let go of the power and the fortune that the family brought them. For some, their lives were ended prematurely.

Many of his close colleagues had found it hard seeing him go and still made trips to the country to visit him discreetly. He enjoyed their company every now and again but didn't appreciate the attention it brought upon him. After all, the Giordano's had enemies and in the act of retiring outside of the family's stronghold he had made himself a fairly accessible target.

It had taken The Phoenix six months of hard graft to train Jack. In that time they performed an astonishing nineteen hits which, even for The Phoenix, had been a formidable task. After six months, he had readily handed over the keys to this lavish penthouse to Jack and slipped away to his retirement retreat. Jack still consulted with him regularly and kept him well versed on the family's affairs, using the older man's knowledge of individual family members to judge his own reactions to situations as and when he felt it appropriate.

"Tony, pick up if you're there," said Jack to The Phoenix's answer phone.

There was a rattle as the receiver was lifted from its cradle.

"Jack, is there a problem? You sound agitated," came the delayed response.

Jack relayed his current situation in full detail to Tony. If there had been a way to politically manoeuvre through this mire without Jack putting himself in serious jeopardy, Tony would be the only man Jack knew who would be aware of it.

"Do you think I'm right?" asked Jack outlining his potential solution.

"I know you are good friends with Stephan, but keep an eye on the bigger picture Jack. If you choose to do this for him, be careful his problems don't come back to bite you. I've seen it happen too many times before Jack. Don't get dragged down by the greedy son of a bitch, okay?" These were Tony's harsh, but honest words of advice.

"Okay, I understand. Thanks for the advice, Tony" replied Jack and slowly replaced the handset.

Jack made a few more calls before pouring himself some bourbon. He sat at his desk in his large leather upholstered chair, from where the fate of many a gangster had been decided. He weighed up the options.

Meanwhile, Stephan was sitting downstairs in the casino restaurant tucking into a freshly caught lobster, his mind cleared of all that had been troubling him for some months. He felt relaxed and was enjoying his meal. Normally, he wouldn't eat alone, but he understood that Jack was sorting out his problems so he would comply. As it drew towards 10:00 p.m. he called over the maître de.

"I'm going to retire to the bar. Don Giordano will be joining me. Would you organise the appropriate drinks, please?"

The maître de nodded and replied,

"Of course, sir."

Stephan sauntered through to the bar. Various people stopped to greet him on the way. He was well known in Chicago and one of the few favourites tipped to take over the whole organisation one day. At 10:10 p.m. the Don arrived in sombre mood. He dismissed his minders at the door. This was *his* territory. Stephan rose to greet his uncle.

"Don, it is good to see you," he said.

"Where is Jack?" was his only response.

"He asked me to tell you the problem is being taken care of and he will join us shortly," said Stephan, at which moment Jack himself entered the bar. "Ah, in fact, here he is already, Don."

The Don looked around to see Jack strolling in, his arms outstretched with a welcoming smile.

"Don Giordano... it's good to see you," he said warmly embracing the Don.

"You too, my son," replied the Don.

Stephan, as with other members of the family, had to get used to the familiar greeting that the Don and Jack shared; a unique greeting that wasn't given to any other member of the family.

"I have made arrangements. The problem will be sorted this evening. You have my word," whispered Jack.

"I have come to rely on you these past five years, Jack. I thank you," replied the Don sincerely.

The drinks were quick to arrive. The finest cognac available in America and an array of fat Cuban cigars were laid out on a wooden platter for their consumption. The Don had fought tooth and nail for years to ensure that his family would receive the best of everything, and felt no guilt at reaping his just desserts. For the next hour, three of the most feared men in Chicago, sat and spoke about everything from business to baseball, the only indication of their position in society being that of the refreshments lavished upon them. Interestingly, Stephan seemed to do most of the talking as the other two sat and laughed at his anecdotes, until eventually the conversation ran dry and a natural pause signified it was time to leave. The Don was the first to rise and the other two obediently followed suit.

"Jack, come and see me sometime tomorrow. There's something I wish to discuss with you," he said.

"Of course, Don," he replied.

"Stephan come here," The Don said playfully. "I have enjoyed this evening very much," he said and, holding the sides of Stephan's head in his hands, he kissed him hard.

"Stephan, I'm going to Ritzy's Nightclub with Vinny. Would you like to join us?" asked Jack. "Vinny's got a few dames lined up," he added.

"Yeah okay, why not?" he replied.

Stephan walked with Jack to the waiting car and the Don gave a glancing wave from the rear seat of his limousine as his own car rolled passed them.

Both Stephan and Jack stood outside the well-lit entrance of the casino as their car pulled up. Vinny was in the driver's seat. He wound down the window.

"Come on, Jack. We're late," he shouted impatiently.

"Okay. Do you think we can fix Stephan up too?" asked Jack.

Vinny winked at Stephan.

"No problem."
They got into the car and Vinny drove off, heading towards the city.

"Oh shit!" said Jack, his eyes rolling. "Vinny, can we detour to the dock warehouse? I've got to pick something up for the Don."

"Jesus Jack, give me a break, I don't want to keep the girls waiting," replied a frustrated Vinny.

"Don't worry, it'll only take a minute."

"Okay... Okay..." Vinny looked to Stephan in the rear view mirror. "Stephan, how do you want your woman tonight?" he chuckled, picking up his mobile phone.

"Blonde and ripe as a vine," said Stephan trying to picture his ideal woman.

Vinny dialed the number to Ritzy's and waited for a reply.

"Hey, George. It's Vinny, can you add an extra woman in tonight?" he asked. There was a pause. "Yeah, that's right we'll be a bit late. Blonde and ripe as a vine. Okay, cheers." He hung up. "The orders in, you got Diane. She's a peach!" laughed Vinny as they approached the warehouse.

As the car pulled up alongside the entrance, Jack was the first to get out. Not wishing to hold up their evening, he hurried over to the door and fumbled with some keys. Vinny heard him curse as he tried to make contact with the lock.

"Stephan, bring me a torch," Jack shouted over to the car.

"It's in the boot," said Vinny, shutting off the engine and passing Stephan the keys.

Stephan took the keys and got out of the car. He walked around to the rear and saw Jack looking over his shoulder towards him.

"We really ought to get some sort of lighting installed out here," he said and continued fumbling with the keys.

Stephan unlocked the boot. He didn't hear Vinny get out of the car. He raised the lid and noticed the light didn't come on. He resorted to stroking the inside with his hands but all he could feel was a plastic surface. *That's odd,* he thought. He turned to call Jack, but Jack was already standing over him.

"Goodbye, Stephan, old friend," he said quietly as he squeezed the trigger on his silenced revolver. A muted thud was the last noise Stephan would hear as the weapon exhaled a streak of smoke from its barrel. Jack watched as Stephan slumped forward, his torso finding the inside of the boot, his legs left draping over the rear bumper. He could never have known what hit him. Jack walked calmly to the passenger's side and got into the car. Vinny wrestled Stephan's legs securely into the boot before joining him.

He looked at Jack.

"I know that was hard for you, Jack. But, he was a bad apple, my friend." He turned to the road and started to drive. "I'll drop you at Ritzy's and join you later."

They were silent for a while before Jack turned to Vinny.

"Vinny, why the extra woman?" he asked.

"It put Stephan at ease for a minute and now they'll put me at ease all night," he laughed.

Jack couldn't help but burst out laughing, as they travelled back into Chicago.

"You know the Don has a lot of respect for you, Jack?"

Jack looked across at Vinny, poker faced and focussing on the road, but said nothing. "I do too," Vinny continued. "I've got to ask though, why is it you've never taken Natasha out? I've seen the way you look at each other."

Jack was quite surprised and replied,

"She sure is beautiful. I don't think I could do her justice, though," he replied curiously. "Besides, when we first met, you said, I'd do well to stay away."

"Shit Jack. That was five years ago. I say that to everybody who asks who she is. I mean; she's the Don's pride and joy. All that he has left of his wife since those bastard Garcia's took her away from us," he snarled, recalling painful past events.

"I'm not sure I could be faithful while going out with the Don's daughter," he laughed.

"Shit, I think you would have to be faithful!" said Jack.

"You English guys really crack me up. You couldn't take a mistress," said Vinny. "That's the Italian way!" he added.

"So, what ever happened to loyalty?" asked Jack.

"The loyalty is for the Don," Vinny replied sternly.

Vinny pulled up outside Ritzy's and asked, "So, you gonna wait for me?"

"Yeah I'll be around." Jack was about to shut the door and he turned back. "By the way, who is my date?"

"George will set you straight, Jack," said Vinny. "Don't worry."

"Okay. I'll see you later."

Jack closed the door and walked towards the club. The two burly men at the entrance opened the door.

"Welcome, Mr Shaw."

"Thank you," he replied and entered the club. There weren't many places that Jack could go without being recognised in Chicago. Unfortunately, he couldn't always remember other people's names. Faces though, he never forgot.

He saw George talking to one of the customers at the bar. As he approached, George saw him and immediately said,

"Mr Shaw, welcome to Ritzy's. Can I get you a drink." he asked humbly.

"Sure... Bourbon," answered Jack who felt he was being watched by the man George had been conversing with.

"Who's that guy, George? I've not seen him here before."

"That guy?" he replied looking over to a figure at the end of the bar, hunched on a stool. "He's some small time crook, just out of the nick. Do you think you could find any work for him?"

"I'm here for pleasure, George. What's his name?"

"Brett Smith. Should I send him over?"

"Get me every detail about him first. Perhaps I'll see him later. Now back to business, who's my girl tonight?" asked Jack.

"Over there, table fourteen." He gestured to a dark corner of the club. "Natasha's her name. You won't be disappointed," said George confidently.

"Okay. Send me over another bourbon and one of whatever she's drinking," he said looking to the table in the corner. All he could see was a pair of slender legs extended out of the side of the table cubicle, a wall concealing the rest of her.

Intrigued, he sauntered over towards the table.

"Jesus!" he exclaimed. "What are you doing here? Did Vinny put you up to this?"

"No, why? Are you disappointed?" replied Natasha, the Don's daughter.

"No of course not, Natasha. But why are you here?"

"Papa thought you might need a friend tonight. I'll leave if you want," she said feeling offended at his reaction.

"Natasha, you shouldn't be here. Come on, I'll take you somewhere more appropriate for a drink," he said holding his hand out to her.

"Okay. Where should we go?"

"We can go back to the casino and have fun being treated like royalty," said Jack.

"Papa doesn't allow me in the casinos," she replied.

"But he allows you to roam strip joints?" Jack replied sarcastically. Looking to the heavens he added, "Only in America!"

Natasha giggled as she looked into his eyes the way she had a hundred times before. But, this evening, there was no chaperone, so she felt more relaxed behaving in the way she felt. *Vinny should be here but he's not,* she thought.

"Where is Vinny?" she asked.

"He'll be here later, but we're not staying one more minute, so the hell with him!" he stated, wanting to remove her from the club without delay.

She felt warm and wet with Jack. He had a self-confidence that she didn't see around the family. They all walked on egg shells around the Don, all except Jack. Jack was also unlike the others in that he was a gentleman. He seemed to actually care about her feelings. He wanted to shade her from the grim realities of the real world, she felt secure...

"Mr Shaw, are you going already?" asked a bemused George.

"Yes, if you could tell Vinny I've taken Natasha home."

"But what should I tell Brett?" asked George.

"George, another time perhaps," he said and he ushered Natasha out of the club.

They didn't talk much in the taxi, as Jack was running through the evening's options in his mind. It would be hard to resist Natasha if she made a move on him. He had fantasised on many occasions about making love to her. But he felt it would jeopardise his future in the organisation. Better simply to see how the evening turned out and allow her to take any lead.

"So, what possessed the Don to send you to meet me there?" he asked tentatively, wondering whether the Don actually had any clue as to her whereabouts.

"Oh don't be silly, Jack. He knows we are in love."

Jack almost choked on his own saliva and tried to change the subject.

"Why doesn't he allow you in the casino then?"

"He feels that gambling is an addiction for weak people. You live above the casino in Tony's old pad don't you?"

Jack, although used to dominating women, was becoming increasingly uncomfortable with the feeling that he himself was being pursued.

"You know exactly where I live. Let's go and shoot some craps and then I'll take you home," he said ignoring her advances.

"No. Let's go up to your apartment and drink some champagne," she said leaning towards him and stroking the side of his cheek.

"Natasha this is ridiculous. I'm going to take you home." he said attempting to assert some authority on the situation.

"Papa wouldn't be happy to hear that you treated me this way," she replied with a mischievous look that Jack felt might spell trouble.

"Okay, one drink!" he said adamantly.

"Oh, Jack. I've never seen you angry before," she giggled moving up close to embrace him.

God give me strength, he thought out loud as they continued on to the casino. He could see the taxi driver smirking in the rear view mirror having followed the whole conversation, like a soap opera.

11 – Infiltration

Benny nudged Greg, who had fallen asleep reading The Phoenix's file. He orientated himself and, showing his embarrassment, quickly closed the file that lay open on his lap.

"Lucky you're not flying commercial really, isn't it?" said Benny smugly looking at the file marked TOP SECRET in large red letters. "We'll be landing soon, so you'll need to buckle up again."

Benny moved across to Harvey. "Come on, Harvey. It's time to land."

"Oh, thanks," he said. Rubbing his eyes he looked over to Greg who was frantically shuffling papers into his case and smiled as if to say, glad you're in the land of the living.

"You'll be met by the FBI as we land. I'm afraid you don't have clearance to enter the hangar," Benny remarked.

They hadn't been told the destination airfield, but clearly they would be landing at a military airfield. Neither would have imagined the VC10 would be taking them to the notorious and secret airbase, namely, area 51.

The clunk of the landing gear being lowered signified their final approach and the tannoy crackled. *Gentlemen, I'm glad to say we're now in contact with the airfield and will be landing shortly. We hope you've enjoyed your trip with us.* Wing Commander Ferrous sounded tired and would find himself a bed soon after landing.

Within minutes they could see the nine large hangars of the airfield that guarded the latest weapons of stealth technology.

The VC10 made a sharp banking turn into its final approach and not before long, they felt the bump as the wheels made contact with the tarmac. The noise within the aircraft increased dramatically as the captain began slowing down the plane to a halt.

Ferrous took instructions from the air traffic control tower and rolled the plane slowly on to its allotted, spot on. Harvey watched from his seat through the small oval window as an array of cars with flashing lights chased across the airfield to meet them.

"Here comes your escort," said Benny peering out of the window.

Greg and Harvey both got up from their seats and gathered their bags together.

"Is it okay to go up front and say goodbye to the lads?" Greg asked Benny.

"Sure, go ahead. It will take me a few minutes back here to crank open the door."

Greg and Harvey made their way to the cockpit to thank the crew for the flight, promising to buy them all a drink if they saw them during the detachment. It was little more than polite lip service though as they would both be travelling on to Chicago.

They soon returned to the main door where Benny was waiting, enjoying the fresh warm Nevada air that had started engulfing the cabin. He was conversing with a suited man who had climbed the steps and was waiting at the door.

"Mr Walters, Mr Bickley." The man nodded his greeting. "Good evening. Would you follow me please?" It wasn't a question, more an instruction.

They looked at Benny.

"Thanks for all your help," said Harvey and Greg nodding. "Yes. Cheers, Benny." And they followed the FBI man out of the plane towards the awaiting cars.

"You look like you're perking up a bit," Harvey said.

"Just glad to have my feet back on the ground," replied Greg still feeling ashamed at his lax in security on the plane.

"Okay, we're going to get you to Chicago and start the briefing from there," said the anonymous man anxiously.

"Do I sense a problem?" asked Greg.

"You might say that. Everything's on hold. Our latest plant, Brett Smith, was murdered earlier this evening. We think we may have a mole."

"Shit..." said Harvey. The stark reality of the danger he had volunteered himself into suddenly hitting home. "What went wrong?"

"We have no idea. His story and record were unquestionable. We think there must have been inside information somewhere."

Greg slumped back in his seat, now alarmed by his own security breach. *Thank Christ I was on a military plane,* he thought to himself.

"Well if you think you're sending me in until you've got this sorted, you've got another thing coming!" said Harvey clearly unnerved by the news.

"We've changed the travel arrangements. We'll be travelling on by car from here. It's a twenty eight hour straight drive. But it's better that way rather than running the risk of being spotted by the Giordano gang's scouts around the airport. No one will know we're coming," said agent Jim Forbes attempting to put Harvey's mind at rest.

Greg looked at Harvey not relishing the thought of an additional twenty eight hours sitting in a car. Harvey responded with a shrug.

"Well if it's going to keep the operation under wraps, then I'm all for it. But we're going to need to get changed first," he said looking at his military green flying suit.

"That's no problem," replied Jim. "We'll travel casually. I'm going to take us to a motel now so we can freshen up. Rob, that is agent Rob Clancy, is going to commandeer a camper truck for us to make the journey slightly more bearable."

Harvey and Greg once again traded looks, seemingly impressed with the agents' efficiency.

They travelled in two cars; Jim taking Harvey and Greg, Rob travelling separately and quickly disappearing in the opposite direction to hire the camper.

They arrived at the twenty four hour motel and Jim went ahead to hire a room. He returned with the keys to a single room in which they would quickly change and freshen up before Rob caught up with them and their new mode of transport.

"Throw of a coin to see who gets the shower first?" Greg asked looking at Harvey.

"Yeah, tails never fails," said Harvey.

Greg flicked the coin.

"Corny... Heads you lose!" he cheered.

The room was simple enough with its single bed, a small table and chair and a television. The bathroom was basic with a mini bath that doubled as a shower.

Back in the main room, Harvey took up residence on the bed and began flicking through the television channels. Jim had arrived with his newspaper and was demoted to the table where he started thumbing through the pages for any interesting news.

"So what do you think really happened?" Harvey asked Jim.

"It's hard to say. There have been so many gangland killings since we put away Gotti. Everybody has been juggling for position. Suspicions are running high on all sides. I don't know what you've been briefed, but we were intending to put you in as high profile as possible. But the thought at the top has changed and we may be better long term getting you in less conspicuously. We can still help you along in building your reputation with you on the inside," said Jim looking at Harvey unenviably. "But last thing I heard was, it's all gone to review. We may in fact be taking you to a non-starter. Let's wait and see, eh?"

"Two days travel for a non-starter? God I hope not!"

"Your safety will be highest on the list of priorities when they make their decision, Harvey. You got any family?" asked Jim.

"Yeah, wife and two kids. You know, the average bundle," said Harvey. "How about you?"

"Divorced. But my two boys are going through college right now," said Jim sadly. "How do they feel about you doing this job?"

Greg walked back into the room right on queue for Harvey to body swerve any more questions.

"Okay, it's all yours, buddy," he said feeling refreshed.

"Right, I'd better get on with it," Harvey said looking across to Jim. He was relieved at having an excuse not to reply to Jim's question.

"Any sign of Rob yet?" Greg asked.

"Don't worry. He'll be along soon," replied Jim watching as Harvey manoeuvred towards the bathroom. *Poor bastard,* he thought.

Harvey got on with it, aware that time was of a premium. Ordinarily he would have preferred to take a long hot soak to revive his aching muscles, but given the time available and on seeing the size of the bath he opted for a shower. Standing under the piping hot jets of water, he began thinking of what Jenny, Rob and Chloe might be doing at that moment. Harvey's mind was still working on UK time. It would be about two a.m. at home. He wondered if Jenny would be having a sleepless night, the first in a long time that she had to sleep alone... the first of many.

"Harvey," Greg yelled from the other room. "Rob's back with the camper. Makes the old Volkswagen Camper look like a Mini Coupe."

"Be out in a minute," Harvey replied reaching out of the shower for his towel.

"Right, Greg. What's all the fuss about?" asked Harvey as he came back into the main bedroom.

Greg pointed outside towards the parking lot.

"Look at the size of that thing," he said in astonishment.

Harvey looked out at the huge camper.

"Wow, I guess maybe this trip won't be so uncomfortable after all!" he said in awe of the huge wagon astride two parking spaces at the front of the motel.

"Rob and I will have to share the driving so it'll be necessary for us to get our heads down between stints," said Jim pre-empting any scramble over his position for one of the bunks.

"Is it a surveillance truck?" asked Harvey looking at the array of aerials. Rob laughed.

"No. That's for the satellite television."

"Don't see anything like this in the UK," replied Harvey as they exited the motel room and went across the car park to meet with Rob and board the camper.

"Enough about the wagon, gentlemen. It's nothing special. Let's get on with it," said Jim impatiently climbing aboard.

They all followed suit; Greg and Harvey opting to explore while the two agents took their posts as driver and navigator in the front.

Down the back, Greg and Harvey looked at each other like excited children discovering new toys.

"Will you just look at this," said Harvey in amazement looking at his new surroundings. The 1985 Honey Honey was an impressive vehicle by UK standards, but fairly run of the mill as an American tourer. At the rear end of the cabin stood a large double bed. Harvey's eyes scanned the interior past the kitchenette with all its mod cons. There were two full length sofas which, they would discover, doubled as beds and an array of electronics from the state of the art satellite TV to music systems and some form of CB radio. Even the front seats could swivel 360 degrees to extend the main cabin area.

"Christ," said Greg. "It's nicer than my apartment back home," he exclaimed opening a door to reveal the on-board toilet facility.

"It would do wonders for the morale of the lads doing stakeouts in something like this, don't you think?" laughed Harvey, imagining proposing this idea to the bosses at the acquisitions department back home.

"Just a little bit conspicuous, Harv," replied Greg enjoying the banter.

"Listen. Why don't you two children get some shut eye? This is going to be a long haul," sounded the thundering voice of Jim at the front, clearly wondering what all the fuss was about.

Greg and Harvey exchanged smirks before regaining their composure; "So what are we in UK time, Harv?"

"Hmmm...about three a.m., I reckon. In fact, I could use some shut eye."" He started arranging the cushions on the sofa in preparation for some sleep, his mind slipping back to the UK, again wondering whether his family would be sleeping soundly in his absence.

"We'll leave the double bed for you guys, since you are doing all the driving," Greg shouted to the front, but

Jim and Rob were too busy route planning to acknowledge, and so Greg retired to his sofa.

"So, are you alright up here, Rob?" asked Jim as he folded away the maps.

"Yeah, no problem. I think we have got the route licked already, you go and rest, Jim. I'll call you when I need you." With that, Jim nodded and ventured to the rear to get some rest.

They didn't stop often, just for fuel and to swap over drivers. Rob drove as far as Colorado before stopping to buy food and provisions. After he relinquished the driver's seat, Jim immediately took over and Rob quickly passed out on the main bed until they stopped again briefly in Iowa where the roles were reversed once more.

Meanwhile, Harvey and Greg had their respite and were now busying themselves mastering the satellite channels, like children in awe. The amount of channels available to US viewers were outstanding compared to the four lousy channels they were accustomed to back in the UK.

As they approached the outskirts of Chicago, Jim and Rob swapped one final time and Jim came over to brief Greg and Harvey.

"Okay guys. Initially, we will be going to a safe house to get properly rested and freshened up. Then, no doubt, the boss will want to come and brief us on the up to date intelligence".

"Thank God," said Harvey, the novelty factor of their transport with all its mod cons long since worn off. "I am beginning to go stir crazy in this box."

"You see what luxury does to people?" remarked Greg. "He's gone soft already," he continued, smirking at Harvey.

"Whatever," said Jim, dismissing the flippant comment. "It will be the same as before. We will be dropped off at the house and Rob will go dispose of the wagon. I don't need to remind you of the facts," he said sternly. "We are in the war zone now, so no fucking about. Alright?" Greg and Harvey both nodded in silent agreement.

They pulled up outside 2068 W. Farwall Avenue and Harvey looked out from the vehicle's tinted window at the nineteen twenties cream coloured building.

It was quite a grand home comprised of three apartments knocked together into one residence. The FBI had acquired the property for use as a safe house in the early eighties, using it for high risk government witnesses. It seemed ideal at the time and in a good area with its quiet tree lined street. There was a clear sight line all around enabling the occupants to observe approaches and if necessary be prepared for any unwanted visitors. Positioned in an upper class area of the city, the location in itself would deter most unscrupulous mobsters from attempting any attack.

The property, having been purchased with most of its furniture after the death of the previous owner, was more than adequate for their needs.

"The door key is this one," Jim said holding out a key that was part of a bunch on a tagged key ring. He passed it across to Harvey. "Just act naturally and make your way up to the house," said Jim. "I'll be right behind you."

Harvey's nerves were finally alerting him to the fact they had reached their destination. The stark reality that he would soon commence the gargantuan and perilous task of infiltrating the Giordano mob sent shivers spiralling down his spine.

"Here goes," said Harvey opening the side door of the motor home. He climbed down to the pavement, relieved to be able to stretch his legs in the open air and on solid ground once more. He lifted his bag and started towards the house. His imagination ran wild, expecting at any time to see an assailant jump from the street as they so often do in the movies. But there would be nobody there.

Greg followed on behind, scanning the streets. Jim temporarily remained in position, keeping a watchful eye while discussing arrangements with Rob for a rendezvous. He would soon leave the vehicle and join Harvey and Greg, who by now, were both already in the building.

"First time in a safe house, eh, Harv?" said Greg admiring the Mediterranean decor inside.

"Yes, I think I can live with this for a while," Harvey agreed as he made his way up the main staircase.

"Fellas, make yourselves at home. It looks like we'll not be having any visitors until tomorrow," called Jim from the hallway.

Harvey quickly found the main bathroom. With separate shower, Jacuzzi bathtub, toilet, bidet and matching 'his and hers' sinks. It dwarfed the motel room where they had last had the opportunity to shower. He passed through another door into what was the master bedroom, where he found the double bed that he would occupy over the coming months. The room had two large windows allowing it to soak up the massive rays of natural light; one overlooking the garden at the rear of the building and the other towards the neighbouring house. He placed his bag down on the bed and went looking for Greg.

Greg had found his own bedroom adjacent to the sun room. Harvey entered to find him looking into the mirrored closet door, grooming himself shamelessly.

"Okay Romeo," he said. "Have you found a kettle yet, or have you been too busy poncing about trying to hide those grey hairs?" he laughed.

Greg did a double take at the mirror, on the one hand startled by Harvey's entrance, and on the other, wondering if his friend was teasing him.

"I don't have any grey hair. Do I Harv?" he asked, examining his scalp closely. "Harv...?" He looked up but Harvey had already gone in search of a kettle. "Bastard!" he mumbled to himself.

Jim walked into the kitchen to find Harvey who, having already located the kettle, was busily hunting around through the cupboards to find some coffee.

"I see you don't waste any time. You should find some coffee in the cupboard by the fridge. The china tends to live in the dishwasher. Most people who use this place aren't too domesticated. Every now and then, the smell encourages someone to turn it on, but it rarely gets emptied."

Harvey thought, *what a contrast*, the state inside the cupboards being filthy compared to their clinical and grand external appearance, appearances so often being deceptive. He fumbled around in the dishwasher to find some half clean mugs, his home life back in the UK now feeling very distant, and his mind considering the dangers that lay ahead.

12 – Love of an Assassin

It had been an evening that Jack would never forget, awkward on so many levels. His professional approach to dealing with Stephan had not been completely devoid of emotion. The facts were straight and the job was done, but an inwardly apparent chink in Jack's armour had led him to briefly consider framing and subsequently dealing with another of Stephan's misgivings.

Stephan had seen Lisa Forbes as an interfering number cruncher; a nobody, yet a thorn in his side, capable of exposing him. While he had paid the ultimate price that evening for his misgivings, *she* would never learn of how her interference had almost led her to her own existence being extinguished on that same evening.

Jack had no such escape. His fate was sealed that evening also, though not in a way he might have expected. He was no match for Natasha. She was powerful by proxy, intelligent, attractive and head strong. Relationships in the organization were generally one sided and outsiders who didn't conform or treat their spouses with the dignity and respect which they believed they deserved, were dealt with privately and most often, brutally.

Natasha had teased Jack into submission in order to gain that evening alone with him, a date which in itself, might have been a dangerous undertaking for Jack, had the evening closed with an undesirable outcome for her liking.

Yet Jack *was* fond of Natasha. He had been since his first sighting of her on his arrival in the US, and the result of that evening was as predictable as an act within a play, the outcome predetermined, the journey to the desired conclusion a tease for performers and audience alike.

But there was no audience to please that evening when both Jack and Natasha began going through the rituals of courtship. The playful and provocative antics of Natasha proved to be a mask to her actual naivety. To Jack's surprise, she had saved herself for the one man that she wished to spend the rest of her days with. He was not to know it on that evening, but Jack Straw was to become that man.

In the days and months following that fateful evening, Jack and Natasha spent most of their spare time together. Jack's cautious approach in dealing with Natasha afforded him time to get past the beautiful exterior that first drew his attention, and examine the personality that to most remained hidden from sight. While he remained busy with business, expanding upon his growing reputation within the family, he also began to look forward to his meetings with Natasha and became the single most regular visitor to the Don's residence.

Henry, the Don's butler and main servant, despite his faults, an English romantic, had grown used to Jack's frequent visits. Perhaps as a result of their shared heritage, Henry's mood would be lifted and he would manage a rare smile while Jack was about. Jack would regularly bypass the house and head straight for the gardens on his arrival, waiting for Natasha before leading her out into the vast expanse of land where they could gain some privacy and discuss all things other than the family business. The vast and beautiful landscaped grounds would remind Jack of his own, more modest, but well-tended garden back in the UK, to which he hoped one day he might eventually return.

The Don would often gaze out from his office within the main house, across the gardens at the couple whose regular strolls reminded him of his own younger times. Though he was not able to boast such surroundings during his own courtship, he could recognize the familiar looks that were shared between the couple.

Over the years, he had borne the brunt of Natasha's hard headed nature. In bringing her up largely on his own and without her mother to lavish gifts and affection upon, Natasha had enjoyed enviable beginnings with no shortage of love and protection. The world had truly been her oyster.

The Don was impressed at how Natasha had matured as a young lady in the months since Jack had been seeing her and was aware that the day was quickly approaching when he would need to let go as a father, so that she could blossom as a wife and with any luck, a mother. Though he dreaded the coming of that inevitable time, some may have said it was to be his proudest.

Natasha was no fool. While she had received the best of everything, she had not squandered her opportunities like so many others within the family. She *did* wear the best clothes, but her wardrobes were not over laden. She had excelled in education, but was compassionate to those less fortunate. She had become aware of the family's public reputation at a fairly early age, although the sordid details of how it had been achieved, remained hidden from her. A closely guarded and dark secret with which one day, as the potential head of the family, she would be burdened, and may herself decide wisely to keep from her own children.

Natasha had dreams of travelling the world, something she hoped to achieve later in life, without the need for an ever present entourage of protection. She enjoyed the family estate. The freedom of riding the horses for hours on end within their grounds was her form of escape.

Losing her mother in such dramatic circumstances as a youngster had been traumatic, but her father had been extremely supportive and she loved him dearly. Of course, the feeling was mutual.

It was a beautiful spring morning when Jack finally proposed to Natasha. The family had been expecting an announcement for months, but this hadn't deterred Jack from choosing his own moment. While, to onlookers, the answer might have appeared clear in advance, on listening to his proposal, Natasha had nevertheless made Jack wait painstakingly before agreeing to the partnership of love. She harboured no doubts other than not to lose the woman's prerogative. Jack in turn then asked her to remain silent about the proposal until his return from a business trip which would take him up state for three days. As a gentleman, he wished to formally ask the Don for Natasha's hand before allowing any announcement to be made.

On Jack's return, the family were all smiles. He was collected from the airport by Vinny. It was apparent to

Jack that three days had been torture to Natasha and somebody, somewhere, had let their secret slip. Vinny remained silent on the subject, refusing to put his joyous mood down to anything other than, *the joys of life*. An unlikely mood for a hardened gangster.

As they pulled up at the casino, Vinny opened the trunk.

"Need help with ya bags?" he smiled.

"No Vinny. I'm okay with them, think I'll get a couple of hours rest."

"Okay. I'll pick ya up at six," he shouted out to Jack.

With bags on the sidewalk, Jack closed the trunk, and before he had a chance to ask what was to happen at six, Vinny had dismounted the car clumsily from the curb and driven halfway down the street. A neighbouring driver honked furiously at this ungainly display of driving. Jack looked on and heard Vinny shouting expletives back at the driver on the standard of their own driving. Jack shook his head and smiled before making his way up to the penthouse.

At six p.m. prompt the intercom rang out. Jack had been asleep and was still fairly groggy from his trip.

"Yeah..." he called down to Vinny, who was waiting patiently by the microphone in the lobby.

"Six p.m. Time to go see the Don," replied Vinny glancing down to his watch in an attempt to figure out whether they would make it on time.

Jack pressed the door release button without replying. The buzzer rang out as the internal door unlocked and Vinny made his way up to the penthouse. Meanwhile, Jack, who had spent his return trip quietly working out what to say to his future, potential and unorthodox father in law, poured himself a glass of Dutch courage and started to dress appropriately for the occasion.

On their arrival at the Don's house, Vinny once again glanced down at his watch and a smile of relief began to appear knowing that he had delivered Jack to the house on time.

"New watch?" Jack asked having observed the number of times Vinny had cast a glare at its diamond encrusted face. Vinny said nothing. Though this would be Jack's night, it was never the done thing to be late for an appointment with the Don.

Henry greeted the pair at the front door, his somewhat fatherly eyes meeting Jack's before welcoming them both in to the hallway.

"I'm afraid dinner will be slightly later than originally planned gentlemen," he whispered bowing his head. "Jack, would you follow me please. The Don is expecting you."

Vinny wandered through to the main reception room where an array of drinks was available while Jack followed Henry through to the Don's office.

Henry tapped on the door in a quiet, yet an audible manner and as the husky voice of the Don hailed back, he gestured for Jack to enter. Henry did not enter with him but smiled briefly at Jack.

"Good luck," he whispered, before turning and making his way back down the corridor to see if Vinny required any attention.

Jack briefly paused for thought before entering the office. The Don was standing, staring out of the window as he so often did when observing Jack in the gardens with Natasha. He wore an appropriate dinner suit as he had done so many times previously when entertaining guests at his home. His bearing was one of dominance. There was no doubt of the hierarchy within the room. Still facing the window and without turning he gestured back with his left hand towards one of the chairs on the opposite side of his desk. Jack, understanding the body language, complied without comment. Taking his seat and manoeuvring to make himself comfortable, he waited in silence.

Only ten seconds passed, but for Jack, it seemed like an eternity. His mind was a maze of words, words which he was struggling to remember in an order that he might communicate legibly.

The Don turned slowly. He had been in deep thought. Yet, as he looked up to meet Jack's eyes square on, he smiled as only a Don could. It was a smile that did not give away any inner feelings that appeared comforting, yet was equally able to portray imminent doom to its subject. His face looked drawn.

"I still miss my wife, Jack..." He paused, lowered himself to his seat behind the desk and looked away, fixing his glance on a photograph of his wife with their new born daughter, Natasha. He continued, "It's a lousy business to be married into."

Jack hung on to Don's every word, carefully analysing each movement and action of the Don intensely. He drew breath and was about to contribute to the conversation when the Don chose to continue.

"I have been watching you for some time." He looked and gestured at the window from which he observed so many of Jack's walks with Natasha during their courtship. "And I think you have something you wish to say to me." Jack was unaware if his comment was a statement or a question. The smile deteriorated from the Don's face and he sat in front of Jack now dead pan. He sank back into his chair and attached his hands firmly to the arms rests like an airplane crash victim moments before impact. His knuckles began whitening. He looked up at Jack and waited in silence.

Jack cleared his throat and drew a deep breath.

"Don Giordano..." he continued, "since my arrival in America you have been my guide. It is true, I have very strong feelings and respect for your daughter..." He stalled and thought to himself, *cut to the chase Jack...*

"Don, I would be honoured if you would bless us with your permission to marry." He chose not to beat around the bush and looked deep into the eyes of the Don whose demeanour had not wavered. He searched for some form of response but the silence grew.

The Don rose from his chair, the blood visibly easing its way back into his knuckles, knuckles which had damaged many a body in their time.

"It is time for dinner," he announced breaking the silence but choosing not to acknowledge Jack's statement. His facial features remained dead pan and as he walked around the desk and past Jack towards the door, Jack rose. Confused but compliant, he followed.

Jack could see Henry at the end of the corridor standing at the imposing doors of the main reception room. They walked slowly and in silence until they reached him. Without instruction, Henry reached out for the two large brass door handles, but the Don held out his hand gesturing him to stop. He turned and looked Jack up and down slowly. Reaching out, he slowly placed his hands on Jack's shoulders, his eyes squinting slightly as he measured up the young and handsome man that stood before him.

"Faberge," the Don whispered to Jack.

A bead of sweat appeared on Jack's brow.

"Excuse me…? I don't understand," Jack replied looking across briefly at an equally confused Henry. He cast his mind back to the day of his arrival when he had unintentionally got the better of the Don. He realized this moment was about to be repaid.

There was another brief pause before the corners of the Don's mouth gained altitude. He continued.

"It would be my honour, my son, if you would be the host this evening." Henry's eyebrows arched. This was a moment he would brag about to friends in the years to come and right on cue he instinctively made a second attempt to reach for the handles. The Don nodded in approval and the large oak doors were swung open before them.

Not a second passed before the three men were greeted with a substantial roar of applause. It seemed the entire family and guests numbering possibly a hundred, stood before them. Natasha appeared from within the crowd of guests, champagne flute and bottle at the ready. The Don once again nodded, and she ran to embrace him. The Don, for the first time that evening, allowed the fatherly smile to escape and gestured with his hands for the party to begin.

What followed would potentially be the happiest evening in the history of the Giordano family, a rare moment when all members of the family and their inner circle of friends would be gathered at a single venue. As the celebrations continued through the night, a legion of security and bodyguards would patrol the grounds ensuring the safety of all those within.

Jack and Natasha were married almost three months to the day after the Don had given his blessing. The wedding itself was a very private affair, although one of the family members, editor of the socialite magazine *Gotcha!*, had been granted limited access for a number of carefully selected photographers to produce press photographs of the couple and select members of the congregation for his high profile society magazine. Despite the screening process, one of the photographers would still be ejected from the wedding reception having gone beyond his remit and taken pictures of some distinguished guests without their permission. The infringement cost him his job, the temporary use of fingers on both hands and, once he finally recovered, a period when he found himself unable to work again in Illinois other than as a freelance.

Jack and Natasha had been oblivious to the short lived infringement. For them, the wedding had gone exactly to plan and, following the celebrations and subsequent honeymoon, they wasted little time in producing their own heirs and grandchildren of the Don.

The next few years passed them by very quickly. Jack would still be required to go on brief *business trips*. Natasha never asked as to detail in any manner other than small talk. She had blossomed into a devoted wife and he, a doting husband.

A couple of years after their marriage, they collectively decided to live with the Don at the family residence so he could take part in the upbringing of his grandchildren. This delighted the Don who found it difficult to hide his excitement when they proposed the idea. He had been concerned as to their open living in the city and the implications on his grandchildren's security.

In married life, Jack converted the penthouse at the casino into his place of work rather than giving it up. There he could meticulously plan any business that required his attention in peace. He tried, whenever possible, to keep his work and family life completely separate, concerned about how Natasha might react if she ever discovered his full involvement within the business.

It had been a warm summer's morning when Jack had been scrutinizing the casino accounts as he often did in the penthouse. A telephone call from his homeland disturbed him, an unexpected call, from an unknown gentleman. His phone rang and Jackie, the office girl and casino receptionist, addressed him in a nervous and squeaky voice.

"Mr Shaw, there's an international call for you. I told the caller you were unavailable but he is most insistent," she said.

"Put him through." Jack scowled at her incompetence. He thought to take the call before arranging for her to be fired. The caller introduced himself in a posh English accent and as the conversation continued, the thought of dismissing Jackie faded from his mind, an unusual oversight by a man who adhered to detail. He was totally engrossed by the conversation that lasted only a few intense minutes, yet would haunt him for some time.

13 – Gotcha Magazine

"It's almost old enough to be an antique. You know these waiting room magazines. But I'm telling you, it's him. It's Christian's son right there on the centre pages," she exclaimed into the telephone mouthpiece while waiving the magazine in her hand like a banner at a parade.

There was a brief pause before Jessica continued. "No, I haven't told him." Her voice wavered and took on a sombre tone. "How could I ever tell him now?" She glanced across at a picture of her son Harvey which years earlier, she had hung proudly on her living room wall.

It was three months since Harvey had been sent to America on a work assignment, and as each day passed, Jessica grew steadily more uncomfortable at how long it had been since he had called or written to her.

That morning she had been for her quarterly visit to the dentist, where she underwent laser treatment to return her teeth to the glimmering white that made her smile sparkle and melt the hearts of middle aged men. She had been sitting in the waiting room sorting through the old magazines that were donated by patients. Whilst ferreting for a good read, she had come across an old edition of *Gotcha!* Ordinarily she would have opted for *House & Country* or *Country Life* in which she could browse through the hoards of millionaire mansions up for sale in the country and dream longingly of what she might opt for given the money. But the selection was, in her mind, poor on that day. It seemed that for the most part the dentist's recent clientele must have differing interests from the norm, as the selection was full of socialite gossip and women's health magazines.

Owing to her already healthy lifestyle, she had opted for the former and had come across an article that made her skin turn grey. She had asked the receptionist if she could take the magazine and by way of thank you, had placed a generous donation into one of the charity boxes that sat proudly on the receptionist's bureau. She had remained preoccupied with the content for her entire appointment. Her normal banter with the dentist was non-existent other than to answer questions with a brief "yes" or "no" response.

"Are you ok, Jessica?" asked the dentist as he concluded the treatment. "You appear unusually out of sorts."

"Yes, yes!" she had replied dismissively and promptly left the room without so much as a *by your leave*.

Once home she had read the lead paragraph of the article over and over again.

Jack Shaw and Natasha Giordano were married last weekend at a lavish ceremony hosted at the Giordano family estate. Jack, the managing accountant at the Giordano group of casinos, is the son of Christian and Helen Shaw who were tragically killed in a car accident in the UK.

She could almost recite the article word for word by the time she eventually decided to call the friend and confidant that she played bridge with on Thursday afternoons. The conversation had not helped her in coming to any conclusions, but it had made her feel better to speak to a friend on this taboo subject of so many years previous.

On finally replacing the receiver, she looked at her watch and, feeling slightly less on edge, decided it was time for some lunch. She took one last glance at the picture of Jack and Natasha Shaw in the centre pages before putting the magazine in an overfilled rack where she kept so many old magazines and articles that held memories for her. She strolled into the kitchen and turned on the radio. Finding her favourite music station, she began to prepare herself a salad sandwich.

Later that day she would go and visit Jenny and the children. She would stay with them overnight as the return journey was too arduous for her to complete in one day. On the train she would read the newspaper but there was nothing out of the ordinary; banks announcing record profits, ministers defending tax rises, the latest scandals involving overpaid footballers and an article about the Vatican. It seemed they were sending an envoy to raise the spirits of the British congregation. Jessica would not read as far as the sports pages but would glance briefly through the television listings just in case there was anything of interest to watch and discuss with Jenny later that evening.

Jenny had been waiting obediently at the platform. Having grown used to her husband's obsession with time keeping, it had slowly rubbed off on her. Since Harvey had left for America she had grown accustomed to Jessica's regular stopovers and enjoyed the company, discussions and updates on what was occurring in the capital around where Jessica was living. Jenny had been brought up in the countryside and was not a great fan of the speed at which large cities operated. The hustle and bustle of commuters and pedestrians hurrying around the streets coupled with the effects of the visible smog often made her feel dizzy. She preferred to listen to Jessica's version of what went on rather than go to the trouble of visiting the capital and feeling its overwhelming effects first hand.

On that particular day she sensed that Jessica was out of sorts, arriving at the station in body but not in her soul which clearly was on duty somewhere else. Jenny wondered if her mother in law's absent minded disposition was merely a symptom of her son's continued absence or something more sinister.

Either way, she felt sure her own news, which she would savour a while beneath her broad smile, would cheer Jessica's spirits.

It wasn't until later that evening, once they had eaten dinner and the children had been tucked away in bed, that they would have a chance to catch up. Jenny would enthusiastically share news that Harvey would be coming home within the month. She hadn't wanted to say anything in front of the children as it wouldn't have been the first time such news had been given and his leave subsequently revoked at the last possible moment.

On this occasion she was filled with hope. It was Greg Bickley's office that had called and explained to Jenny that while Harvey might be expected to carry out an assignment while home, his leave was assured and any infringing assignment would be compensated in lieu time.

Jenny still felt unable to throw caution to the wind and let the children know *daddy* was coming home, but she was visibly excited at the prospect and while induced with wine from dinner, she was unable to contain her enthusiasm. She relayed the news with smiles and in a highly excitable tone to Jessica.

They both talked about Harvey and reminisced over past family outings for a couple of hours before the euphoria finally waned. They drank several more glasses of wine between them before turning their attention to the television. Sometime later Jessica, fidgeting on the sofa, bored by the dulcet tones of an ITN newsreader, interrupted the program by turning to Jenny. She put her hand on the younger woman's arm and, in a rather down beat tone, took her into her confidence.

Jenny had not been paying much attention to the television either. Instead she had been thinking of nothing other than the return of her husband. The sudden change in tone took her somewhat by surprise yet, she found herself quickly spellbound as her mother in law spilled out in great detail a revelation from her past. At the end of each verbal chapter Jenny took on board another mouthful of wine while considering some form of response. She struggled to make sense of the entire episode of Jessica's life.

"...and so you see? How can I possibly tell him now?" Jessica concluded reaching for the wine bottle topping up Jenny's glass followed by her own.

"Jessica," Jenny said finally, tilting her head to one side and looking into her mother in law's eyes. "You must have known that I can only advise you to do one thing?" The wine providing Jenny with a masterful confidence.

Jessica said nothing.

"You must tell him as soon as you can. He has a right to know and you cannot continue to burden yourself." Jenny's original curiosity now turning to anxiety as she realised she had been drawn in on this dark family secret. Feeling like an unwilling co-conspirator, she continued, still riding high on the alcohol that was warming inside her, she stated firmly, "You must tell him the day he arrives from America."

In time Harvey *would* forgive his mother for not having imparted to him the true identity of his father much earlier in his lifetime, but, initially, on hearing this revelation, curiosity would get the better of him and he would immediately embark upon a quest to learn of the family he never had.

14 – Long Haul Home

Greg Bickley and Harvey Walters were busy packing their belongings as their assignment in the US was almost complete. Though their tour hadn't directly led to any major arrests, it had been seen as a great intelligence success which had *continued to demonstrate the value of international cooperation on such investigations,* according to the post operation report.

It was largely Harvey's naivety and curiosity that led him to volunteer for the tour on Special Ops. Such assignments were few and far between, and he felt it would open doors for career moves later on in life.

It was not long after his arrival in the US that he had concluded such assignments were better left to younger individuals who had no emotional ties. He would be relieved to return to the UK, deciding that assignments which led to family separation, albeit for their own safety, were not for him.

The months had passed slowly and, though he had hardly been able to communicate with the outside world, he had always kept a picture of his wife and children concealed upon his person.

He had been fortunate that this valuable reminder of home had remained secret from the individuals he had reluctantly spent the last six months with. They were anything but trusting. Had the small passport sized photo of Jenny and the kids been discovered, the suspicious minds of his newfound counterparts would have left Harvey Walters, aka *Bill Moore,* to have been brutally removed from their inner circle like others who had preceded him with less fortunate endings.

Harvey had no intention of joining those others, most of who were believed to be incarcerated forever within the foundations of Chicago's sky scrapers, and other such buildings built with mob money.

He *had* been cautious. Aware of the possibility of discovery, he had dreamt up a fictitious account of who the individuals in the picture were and what they meant to him. Thankfully, he never had the need to spell out his story and now, on leaving the country, felt relieved that his rather shaky piece of fiction had never been tested.

Greg and Harvey would leave the country in the same manner by which they arrived; collected quietly but routinely by US agents and delivered back to Area 51, where they would join the crew of another RAF transport plane which would, in turn, deliver them home to the UK.

Once in the UK, both Harvey and Greg should ordinarily have been allowed one month's special leave, time given to repatriate and spend with their families. However, as was so often the case, in a cruel twist of fate, this leave would come with catches for at least one of them.

The ComCen Officer at Area 51, had received the Notam signal from the UK the same morning they were due to fly out, and duly notified aircrew officers meeting Harvey and Greg to collect it on behalf of their non-ranking passengers.

APPROVED was the most important word read from the scanned signal. However, further within the message, there was information regarding an unspecified corporate protection role for which one of them, would be required to remain on standby.

It would be a huge kick in the balls considering all that they had done.

"Told you we should have arrested someone," Greg stated glumly, in a bad attempt to make light of the news before sauntering off to find a telephone to call home.

Before boarding the VC10, he called the UK to question the message. He was put through to a member of the HR department who was quick to compliment them on their work, comments that given the rest of the signal, Greg simply took as lip service. The anonymous HR voice went on to outline the possible requirement for one of them to lead a team protecting an Italian dignitary currently touring cities in the UK. Greg was in no mood to haggle. He was tired after the long trip back to Area 51, and simply absorbed as much of the information as possible before hanging up the phone.

He met back up with Harvey in a small military cafeteria where they both drank a sub-standard cup of coffee before departure. They would not be required to attend the pre-flight brief on this occasion and would meet up with the aircrew who were, by this time, already briefed and out on the tarmac busy conducting pre-flight checks. Being second timers and having been given the VIP treatment and tour of a similar aircraft on their way out to the US, their trip home in the old tanker would seem significantly less interesting.

During their coffee, Greg relayed his conversation with the HR department. He emphasized that the additional job was not actually definite and, if required, would only take a couple of days, after which they would be able to return to their much anticipated leave with an extension for time lost.

However, neither was naïve to the reality of a 'non definite job' actually being anything other than a sure thing. Neither man relished the prospect of losing valuable time off once they returned, so they finally agreed to choose their fate with a toss of a coin for the guarantee of an uninterrupted period of freedom.

"Harv, I'm sorry. If I hadn't made plans to be away for my leave I would step in... Sorry," Greg sighed. Looking down at his wrist and the obverse of the coin bearing the shiny head of Queen Elizabeth the second.

Harvey looked deflated. He had been harbouring hopes that even a loss on the flip of the coin might still have left a chance that Greg would indeed have done just that. Greg was an independent man with no one waiting back to greet him in the UK but, he had wasted no time in booking himself a holiday in Europe upon hearing the news of their impending return home. He had been on many detachments and was more aware of what could, and quite often did, go wrong for those returning home.

He had taken the gamble of making himself unavailable expecting any such eventuality not to *crop up* until they were at least back home and within contact of the office. On this occasion the advance signal had produced a less than comfortable near miss. Albeit, if he had lost this gamble, his insurance should have covered his costs, he was nonetheless a great believer in the phrase, *To the victor go the spoils* and would not give an inch to his friend on the subject.

On seeing the obverse face upon his wrist, *his* mood had immediately improved. In his mind's eye he could already see the golden beaches and looked forward to drinking piña coladas during long sunny days while chatting to ladies wearing bikinis laying by a warm swimming pool. These thoughts were comforting to him and while they stood before each other, the coin still resting on the back of Greg's wrist, neither would have any idea that his vacation would be cut short so dramatically in a couple of weeks.

Harvey and Greg stood in silence, each contemplating their own result when their thoughts were interrupted by one of the crew members. With the pre-flight brief completed sometime earlier, the crew member was horrified to see the two of them still in civilian clothes. He ushered them away quickly to find suitable flying clothes before joining the flight engineer and air loadmaster already aboard the plane.

The pilot and his navigator were walking around the exterior of the plane. The next time they would enjoy the clean air, would be on the tarmac back in a damp and rainy Blighty. The pilot impatiently tapped on his watch as Harvey and Greg arrived. They boarded the plane and found their seats being closely followed by the pilot and navigator who headed straight for the flight deck. Already delayed, it would only be a few minutes before the engines would roar and the plane would head at full speed for the blue skies of Nevada. Greg Bickley and Harvey Walters were finally leaving the US in the same discreet manner by which they had arrived.

Conversation on the trip across the Atlantic was fairly minimal as both Greg and Harvey were thinking of the separate paths they would take in the upcoming weeks. The crew were preoccupied in the cockpit and the load master, with the exception of giving out food during the flight, would take time to sleep off a hangover gained from his final night out on the town; an expensive night playing black jack and roulette in the casinos of Las Vegas that had cost him a month's pay.

After several hours, the plane rattled and bumped violently and they had eventually felt the earth under their feet. Harvey Walters opened his eyes. Looking out through one of the windows, he was comforted to see what he hoped were the Home Counties and that they were in their final descent.

He had managed to go to sleep for the majority of the flight soon after the refreshed load master had brought them some food, oblivious to the noise and distinctive smell of the non-commercial flight. Greg was also now rousing. He too had slept through a large portion of the flight. Having taken a row of four seats soon after Harvey had passed out, Greg had made a makeshift bed for himself.

Compliantly sitting in the upright position of his uncomfortable seat, Harvey's fatigue had forced him into a deep state of unconsciousness, yet his compliance would only serve to reward him with a stiff neck for his trouble. Greg, however, had enjoyed a refreshing respite but sitting up appeared unnerved with the rattling of the airplane. He prematurely buckled himself back into a single seat.

Crew members frantically moved around the plane conducting final checks in preparation for landing and the pilot, who had spent the previous five minutes in contact with the air traffic controller in the tower at Brize Norton, turned on the cabin intercom. As with their previous flight, Greg and Harvey were the only passengers and the remote crackly voice asked them informally to buckle up.

It was a bumpy final approach as the large plane was manoeuvred manually through the rain clouds and turbulent weather of Oxfordshire. The landing gear of the plane was finally lowered with the airfield in sight and the familiar loud clunk gave its two civilian passengers a jolt as the wheels fixed into position.

With the airflow under the plane now interrupted by the huge hanging wheels, the noise in the cabin grew louder and the plane rumbled violently as the pilot routinely wrestled the controls and guided his plane through the last remaining mist and down further until the familiar sound of rubber making contact with the wet and weatherworn English runway could be heard.

It was almost midday in the UK and on their arrival in the terminal, Harvey would waste no time in finding a telephone and calling home to speak with Jenny.

Jenny had answered the phone almost immediately, and upon hearing Harvey's voice, she became hysterical with tears of joy. She had not been informed of the exact details of Harvey's arrival, but she had been impatiently marking time in anticipation of this long awaited call. She would drop everything and bundle the children into the car, immediately embarking upon her own journey to collect her husband from the RAF base.

She had still not told the children of their father's return and would leave this to the very last moment, fending off the young children's naïve questioning of the paradox they were faced with in their mother's peculiar mood.

"Why are you crying and smiling at the same time, Mummy?"

Her journey would take more than an hour, but there would be no stops and she would find it difficult to stick to the speed limits during this brief yet agonizing trip towards the long anticipated reunion.

Greg had waited for Harvey while he was using the telephone and they would now both go and spend their last remaining hour together, changing back into civilian clothes before heading off for a brief drink while they waited for Jenny to arrive. Greg would eventually make his own way from the base but felt he would sooner see Harvey safely back into the arms of his family before organizing himself. He hoped being present at their reunion might remove some of the stigma he felt having arrived to take Harvey away from his wife on the day they departed to the US.

His hopes paid off. Indeed, once Jenny had finally let go of Harvey in order that the children could share the hugs with their father, she wrapped her arms around Greg and thanked him for bringing Harvey home safely.

Greg would soon see Jenny again, but the mood of that meeting would reveal tears of anxiety rather than joy.

15 – Conscience

Jack hadn't used the penthouse with as much frequency since marrying Natasha. Yet he had just spent several days in succession discreetly coming and going through the private entrance, choosing to avoid the casino floor. His mind was on a new job ordered by the Don and he did not wish to be distracted.

That week his only contact with the staff had been when he telephoned briefly to order drinks and food, which they would be required to take up to him. They rarely saw him other than that. The reception staff would catch a glimpse of him on his arrival early in the mornings and occasionally on his departure in the evenings. But despite his discretion, the news that he was in temporary residence would circulate amongst the staff like fire spreading through dry woodland. They would all *feel* his presence.

On taking over the lavish apartment, Jack had carried out a number of modernisations including the installation of a slave system to the casino CCTV. He was able to watch *all* the comings and goings of gamblers and staff on the casino floor, from the individual tables to the slots, and the external perimeter of the entire premises. On occasion, he would call down to ask the duty manager to find out who individuals were at certain tables.

The punters fascinated Jack and over the years he had spent a lot of time analysing the mannerisms and body language of the gamblers, from euphoria to desperation. Jack had learned to see through the poker faces that frequented the floor. He knew exactly how most were faring without the need to examine their cards or the colourful gaming chips that sat in front of them like status symbols.

As a known additional *eye in the sky* staff were apprehensive when it was rumoured he was on the premises, harbouring suspicions that each time they passed a camera, their boss might be watching their every move. Their anxiety would often lead to errors of judgment if these periods of anxiety were extended beyond a few days in succession.

The security team was especially nervous of his presence and, while they had a much higher level of rapport with Jack than most other staff, they still viewed his scrutiny as micro management. On occasion, they would deliberately manhandle an innocent bystander out of the casino rather than give Jack the impression they were sitting on their hands. Jack enjoyed their proactive, albeit overzealous, approach to security and, though many an innocent holiday maker had been dealt with roughly in this way; the throughput of punters was robust enough for these indiscretions not to impact on business. Jack saw no harm in this, feeling that it would also serve as a warning to those who might wish to attempt to cheat the Giordanos out of their *hard earned* booty to stay away.

Jack was not interested in the casino comings and goings of that week. He had more important things on his mind and would soon depart to Europe on *other* business. It would be the first time he had returned to his homeland in a decade and he had spent the recent evenings making small talk with Natasha over how he would like her to go with him to the UK in the future.

His better judgment of course stopped him short of extending her an invitation to go with him on this occasion. She had been quietly disappointed not to at least receive an invitation from her husband, but she understood that for him, to mix business and pleasure, would have been quite unacceptable.

Over the years, Jack had shared with Natasha a copious number of stories about the city of London, his family and of course his country home; a home which had remained unoccupied, but maintained to the highest standard for many years pending his inevitable return. News of Jack's upcoming trip would fuel Natasha's enthusiasm to visit his homeland and at her leisure, she began researching what the family might do given the opportunity to take a holiday in the country of her husband's birth.

Jack was pacing up and down in the penthouse. It was almost time for him to begin his journey. He had said his goodbyes to Natasha earlier in the day and had chosen to spend the last few hours of his time in the US revising routes for his impending trip and finalising his plans. He would not write any information down. All the information he required would be stored in his mind's eye.

With all preparation complete, Jack sat staring at his suitcases. He sighed as his mind wandered back to the life he once had in the UK and how, following his stretch in prison, he had been drawn down this fateful path to where he was on that day. He had no regrets about his life. He had achieved what, even then, most of the Giordano family had thought to be not only unachievable, but unimaginable. Jack was almost certain that the path fate had led him down, had prevented him from self-destructing, though as a family man himself now, he was growing weary of the killing.

Now in his mid-thirties, Jack had already tallied up a headcount of over thirty professional hits, including that fateful first hit in Bournemouth. These had all been attributed to The Phoenix, by worldwide law enforcement agencies, the hit man who had become something of a legend within the underworld. Given the overall amount of names and dates contained within the list of believed victims, it was not difficult to understand how he had gained a legendary status. By anybody's reckoning, the list extended beyond the years of any regular mortal.

Jack sat pondering caressing the hardened exterior of the case containing the tools of his trade. Inside was a unique and untraceable weapon created with a single purpose in mind; to be used to extinguish one life, the life of an honest and dignified ambassador, an ambassador of the Roman Catholic Church… A man of the cloth.

Jack was not a particularly religious man though the Giordano family were regular attendees at mass and key donators to church funds. How they could match their morals to ordinary church going folk would remain a mystery to him. The congregations, on the other hand, were great admirers of the Giordano family and grateful for all that their charity had brought to those less fortunate within their communities. The Giordano's had managed to harness a 'Robin Hood' style reputation, largely in recent years due to Natasha; whose genuine, empathetic 'Maid Marion' approach to the community had boosted reverence of the family name.

There would be no name plaque awaiting Jack in heaven, if indeed such a place existed, and he took little comfort in that thought. This most recent job rattled his conscience more so than any other. To seal the fate of a Bishop would surely be a direct attack on any God, an act from which there would be no coming back. It would appear that the crimes on which the Bishop's fate had been decided, were nothing more than to make threats, to tell publicly what he knew about financial dealings within the Vatican bank; a bank in which the mafia had been rumoured to hold a considerable vested interest. He had done no harm to mankind and simply despised the fact the church was being corrupted.

That was all Jack had been told and it was more than he needed to know, more than he *wanted* to know. Yet in knowing, he couldn't help but wonder how these individuals of such high public morals could actually stoop so low as to have this softly spoken and honest man's life snuffed out like that of a common criminal. The order to send the bishop prematurely to meet his maker had come directly from Don Giordano himself, though it was unlikely to be a decision he would have made in isolation. It bore a veiled message that considerable concern was being felt from the top down within the organization and spanning several oceans, concern that somebody believed only The Phoenix could be trusted to eradicate.

Sitting, staring and wondering… time was drawing on. Jack opened the case one last time before leaving for the airport. He meticulously checked each individual piece of the weapon, like a sculptor admiring his work of art, before replacing each into its carved protective resting place and securing the lid.

There would be no Vinny to collect him that day. Only the powerful heads of families were informed of this latest job. Jack would make his way anonymously to an airfield where he would be met by a jet that would in turn, ferry him across the pond to a quiet private airfield in the Home Counties of the UK.

Everything had been arranged. He would reappear in the UK quietly, as though he had never left, not passing through customs, the contents of his cases would remain unhampered. Lucio, whom he had not seen for some considerable time, had arranged everything to perfection and would be waiting to take him to his home.

"Welcome home Jack!" shouted Lucio, attempting to be heard over the roar of the jet engines. Jack had seen the Bentley as they came in to land and had guessed it would be Lucio's. He was unable to hear Lucio's welcome but saw him as he climbed down the few short steps. He had mustered a wave while desperately attempting to avoid the path of the quickly departing plane.

The disembarkation had been very brief. Before the aircraft had even reached to a standstill, the side door had been opened, on board steps were hastily lowered into position and Jack was waved to the door by the navigator who followed behind him solely to expedite his departure. He passed Jack's baggage to him before immediately climbing back aboard. There was a justified sense of urgency on the part of pilot and navigator. On board, the pilot looked back through the curtain that separated the cabin from the flight deck, anxiously searching for his colleague and clearly eager to be on the move again before anybody realised they were off their registered flight path. Jack hardly had time to thank the navigator before the door closed and the plane was heading back down the runway of the deserted airfield, gathering speed for take-off.

Jack turned and approached Lucio with his arms wide open. As the roar of the departing plane faded, the two old friends shared a warm embrace.

"Hello, my friend," Lucio said finally.

Having exchanged greetings the two retreated to the warmth of Lucio's car which was parked on the edge of the runway with its engine already purring. Jack glanced around for Lucio's entourage but there was no one in sight and as he stowed his bags in the boot, Jack was surprised to see Lucio entering the large car via the driver's door. Slamming the heavy boot door closed, he joined Lucio in the front of his Bentley. Lucio stared across at Jack.

"What, you think I can't drive?" he cackled before putting the Bentley into drive and heading towards the exit of the airfield. Jack laughed loudly, apologised and settled himself into the passenger seat of the luxurious vehicle.

They headed out and through the small country lanes of Southern England and Lucio and Jack shared stories of those whom they both knew but neither had seen for many years on either side of the pond. They did not and would not talk of Jack's business on this occasion, almost as though in respect for the latest victim and what needed to be done. The job had been as delicately handled on this side of the Atlantic as it had within the US.

Lucio would take Jack to the house and, though he had not seen it for many years, would find it exactly as the day he had left it. Lucio had indeed done everything he promised to keep the place as it was, knowing that one day his friend would return.

Approximately an hour after they had set off, Lucio reached the driveway of Jack's family's residence. He drove the imposing vehicle onto the drive and the familiar crackle and crunch of tyres grinding gravel could be heard. For Jack the memories began flooding back, the good, the bad and the unthinkable... the times of Jack's youth, an untamed youth that following the death of his parents, went undirected and wasted upon drugs and women.

"Lucio. Do you remember that girl, I think she was called Lee?" Jack asked through morbid curiosity yet knowing exactly what her name was.

Lucio chose to ignore the question and instead, as the tyres continued grinding their way down the length of the drive, he replied,

"Here we are. I hope you will find it just as you left it, my friend."

Jack felt a sense of nostalgia and ignored the lack of response to his question. He peered up at the building that held so many memories. The last time Jack had been in residence, he had been an angry and unfocussed young man and, though more than a decade had passed, he struggled to hide the deep feelings welling up inside him.

Lucio looked across at his friend. They had both visibly aged since their last meeting.

"Jack, here are the keys. We have made sure you have everything you will need." He sensed his friend's unease. "Welcome home, Jack," he concluded softly and pressed the boot release button signifying the end of the journey and the time for them to go their separate ways once again.

Jack opened the heavy door of the Bentley as the boot of the vehicle quietly glided open. He wasted no time in removing his two cases and placed them down by the driver side door. Lucio had not climbed out of the car but instead lowered his window.

"Jack, if you need anything call me." He passed Jack a note with a telephone number. Jack looked at the piece of paper.

"You not coming in old friend?" he quizzed. He had expected Lucio at least to join him for a few hours.

"No, not this time Jack. Call me when it's done." Lucio's window glided up slowly until it was sealed closed. He gave Jack a nod of friendship before turning back to the wheel and manoeuvring the Bentley full circle and back out of the drive.

Jack stood for a moment, took stock of his surroundings and, picking up his cases, moved on towards the front door. He shuffled the key ring full of keys for various doors and closets around the house. It took him a few moments to recall which of them Lucio had held out to him and would fit the front door of his childhood home.

He mustered a reminiscent smile as memories flowed back of past youthful nights when he had fumbled around, drunk and high, attempting to gain access to his house. Those drunken nights were now long past and this night he would seek only two things, one large night cap followed by several hours sleep.

It was four days before the planned hit. He would need to be fully rested before the job, but he would also take the opportunity of this trip to pay a visit to his lawyer's office. He had received a call that had unnerved him before leaving the US. A call that related to family matters, private business which had been playing on his mind and he needed to urgently attend to. But for the time being, no business could keep him from his bed.

Jack Shaw lay in his comfortable four poster bed the next morning, he could hear the familiar sounds of robins chirping away in the garden. Blue tits also fluttered around the trees, calling out to each other, and every now and again their tunes would be drowned out by the familiar dark call of a predatory owl. It was light but still early and Jack did not want to waste any time during his relatively brief trip. He pulled back the bed covers with his right arm and lay still for a moment, allowing the cool air of the bedroom to act as a bodily alarm. It sent his warm flesh into a brief period of shock, goose pimples appeared across his well-tanned body.

He sat up and rubbed his face with the palms of his hands before heading across to the bathroom. He stood staring deep in the mirror that hung above the sink, the face of an assassin staring back. He experienced a brief moment of déjà vu, one of many on this trip. However, this was of a quite real memory, a recollection of a similar moment many years ago, a moment on the day Lucio had called, the day that his life had changed for ever.

Eventually, he turned away and head to the shower. He rotated the large brass taps and climbed in to the cubicle that would incarcerate him for the next few minutes. The glassy doors surrounding him quickly steamed up and his body experienced the thermal reversal as his blood returned to the outer reaches of his soul. He picked up his razor and began removing the thick stubble that had amassed during his lengthy trip.

"Ahh!" he cursed aloud as the razor failed to glide over a small part of his neck but instead removed a layer of skin. The piping hot water swirling around his feet gained a momentary red tint as his body briefly expelled blood in disgust at his clumsy behaviour. He glanced down and cursed but quickly resumed the task until his face was smooth and he finally felt refreshed. He reached out of the cubicle for a towel before returning to the bedroom.

For a moment he thought he sensed a smell of toasting bread in the air, *another déjà vu?* He shook his head and dismissed the thought as wishful thinking. Taking an old pair of slacks from the wardrobe he began to dress, comforted by the fact that his body could still seamlessly fit into this ageing garment. He had an appointment which had his mind preoccupied.

Jack always slept with his bedroom door deliberately ajar. He had always liked it that way as it increased the airflow within the room. It also served to remove any element of surprise for those wishing to approach quietly while thinking him to be asleep. He had been a light sleeper for the majority of his life but the jetlag produced by the twenty four hours travelling, coupled with a large night cap the previous evening, had enabled him to manage a comfortable and unusually deep sleep.

Suddenly, disturbed by an unfamiliar noise coming from the hallway downstairs, Jack stood bolt upright like a soldier on parade. He manoeuvred quietly until his back was tight against the bedroom wall, blinking slowly as a thousand thoughts rushed through his head. He waited, squinting his eyes in an attempt to tune his senses past the silence and on to anything more sinister that might signal an intruder's presence. He could hear muffled movements as though somebody was climbing the carpeted staircase. His relaxed mood of a few minutes previous instantly gave way as the mind-set of The Phoenix instinctively took over. Staring across at the dresser where his nearest weapon of choice would be, he realised he would not have time to reach out without alarming the intruder to his own whereabouts.

He attempted to search beyond the room through the crack of the door but could not manage a clear view of the staircase. With nothing to hand and still only half dressed he silently began removing his thin leather belt strap.

His mind was racing. His only option was to use the leather belt as a weapon to buy him some time so he could make it over to the dresser and retrieve the hand gun. As his mind calculated the possibilities of what might happen next, the door swung open and without a moments delay he lunged forward.

With a belt end wrapped around each hand he took the intruder from behind and pulled the ends tight around their neck. There was a crash as a tray fell to the ground, pieces of china bounced silently off the carpet then collided together loudly before coming to rest, spraying brown liquid across the light coloured carpet. Jack and his intruder now bonded together by the leather strap, both struggling they fell to the ground in a blink of the eye, the intruder letting out a high pitched moan as they cushioned Jack's landing. Jack clearly held the upper hand, his body pressing firmly on top of theirs as the belt strap tightened around their neck. Jack took his first chance to see the face of the intruder and then immediately loosened his grip on the belt. Startled, he lifted his head, his body still embraced against theirs.

"Lee… What the hell are you doing here?" His tone one of frustration and remorse. He looked down at her terrified face and hesitated momentarily, though her eyes were reddened and full of tears, the years had not diminished her beauty.

"I miss you…" she whispered. He released the belt slightly from her neck and gently brushed his hand over her hair. *I loved you once, I thought of marrying you once,* He thought. She took a deep breath and felt relieved that she was in the hands of her once client and lover and she felt safe.

"Why Lee? Why the hell are you here?" Her eyes were apologetic but inviting at the same time. She thought this nightmare would turn into an evening of passion like the many they had shared so often in the past. Her sweets lips aroused and ready but all he could hear and focus on were the parting words of the Don, his father in law. The words echoed inside his head. *You will appear like a ghost and slip away like you were never there. There must be no witnesses my son.*

He wanted her so much but knew the correct thing to do was obey the orders.

"Lee, you should have learned never to visit people without an invitation." The sweetness in her eyes was replaced by a tear.

He continued, "I'm so sorry."
Without further hesitation The Phoenix resumed his grip on the belt.

A solitary tear escaped from the corner of his eye. Falling silently it landed on the cheek of his intruder and past lover. Two tears, his and hers, joined as if in one last symbolic embrace. As the final gasps of breath fought their way from her body, Jack Shaw lowered his face down to hers and kissed her goodbye.

16 – Prostitutes of Law

Harvey Walters had been sitting with his mother in the plush London offices for over half an hour. On their arrival, they had walked up to the reception from street level and been asked to sit in the waiting area.

The plush reception area bore more resemblance to that of a hotel rather than a lawyer's office; with its large Chesterfield sofas surrounding solid wood coffee tables. Portraits of partners past and present adorned the walls.

Before announcing their arrival to the main offices, the receptionist served them with fresh filtered coffee. The reception itself appeared all but empty other than for the receptionist's tip tapping on a keyboard signifying she had returned to her work station behind the tall reception counter.

"This is ridiculous," whispered Harvey to his mother some twenty minutes into their wait, not wanting the receptionist to overhear his comment.

Jessica looked across at him over the rim of her reading glasses and smiled. She had her head buried in a 'Country Life' that had been left on the table amongst a precisely fanned selection of magazines, magazines deemed good enough for *Houghton and Harrow* clientele.

Jessica felt rather privileged to have the latest issue in her hands rather than the usual old donated copy that she had been used to at her doctor and dentist's receptions. She was perfectly comfortable and in no hurry to move. Given the surroundings and the polite staff of the office, she might have stayed the entire morning. Her ease would have pleased the office designers immensely. They had worked their designs revision after revision only one year previously before arriving at one that would deliver an atmosphere suitable for the law firm's employees and clientele. Harvey clearly did not feel the same sense of ease, but had other things on his mind.

He got up and began pacing. An oil painting caught his eye and he decided to examine it closer. Standing before the portrait, he looked up at the pompous individual who appeared from every angle to be glaring back at him.

Unnerved by the clever artistry, he began observing some of the other portraits of other individuals of similar pomp and attire. From one end of the wall he made his way down the entire row of portraiture until he was back at the entrance doors and underneath Mr Francis Houghton, co-founder of the Houghton and Harrow partnership.

Pausing below each portrait, Harvey had seen the same illusion embedded within the eyes of the subjects. The artist had immortalised these figures perfectly. He wondered if the employees found it unnerving having the ghosts of past employers watching each time they walked the length of the corridor or left their desks for a break. A shiver ran down his spine at the thought.

Reading the plaques outlining the internally acclaimed importance of each individual, Harvey realised he was outside of his comfort zone. These individuals lived in a world alien to Harvey's normal life. He noted the lack of women among the paintings, a sure sign of the historical female discrimination during the early days of the law firm's existence. Harvey wasn't aware that he was thinking out loud and as he had stood under each portrait had labelled each individual with a comical yet deliberately demeaning name. Jessica, now fully engrossed in her magazine, was not paying attention to his remarks although the odd giggle from behind the reception counter suggested that his thoughts weren't being wasted.

A door opened down the narrow carpeted corridor beyond the reception counter and Harvey's attention became diverted. The figure of a heavy set man, documents buried under his arm, appeared briefly but made his way in the opposite direction to what Harvey guessed might have been the partnership's board room. Before his direction had become clear, Harvey had forced a smile, looking after him hopefully but, this was not Mr Jones, who was in a different office attempting unsuccessfully to track down the third party invited to the meeting that had been arranged for that morning.

Harvey looked across to his mother and shrugged. His impatient streak had been observed early on in life and the years had not mellowed him. But under the circumstances, Jessica decided that she would forego any further reading and intervene on her son's behalf. She put her reading glasses back in their case and then called across to the receptionist.

"Excuse me," The noise of the typing ceased and a small blonde head appeared over the top of the reception counter.

"Can I help you, madam?" asked the young lady casting her beaming smile across in Harvey's direction.

"Yes. Could you please ask Mr Jones if indeed we are going to have our meeting as it is getting rather late?" she said in a soft voice with a touch of sarcasm.

The young receptionist, unable to interpret the note of sarcasm, simply beamed a manufactured smile back to Jessica and replied,

"Of course," before scurrying off down the corridor to the main offices.

"Do you think he has changed his mind?" Harvey asked his mother.

"Well, maybe his trip was cancelled or something. Don't worry, I am sure we will be informed shortly. After all, you don't go to the trouble of organising a meeting at an office like this and then not show up, do you?"

Harvey looked around at his surroundings and, shrugging his shoulders once more, chose to sit back down. His backside hardly made contact with the sofa before the receptionist reappeared.

"Mr Jones will see you both now," she said. "If you would like to follow me please." She smiled, turned and started down the corridor. Both Jessica and Harvey rose and straightened their clothing before following on behind the girl who led them to Mr Jones' office. She then returned to her own duties in reception.

On Harvey's return from the US, Jessica had plucked up the courage to explain to him about his past.

He was shocked to hear that his father hadn't been at all as portrayed in his earlier years, but rather a man of money, a city slicker involved in many of London's major mergers and acquisitions. Christian had made a good name for himself among colleagues for his tireless efforts in meeting the tight deadlines of highly complex deals and, unlike most of them, he had spent many a long evening working late in the office while his wife remained at home with their only son Jack.

Christian and Helen Shaw had chosen not to reside within the city, rather opting for the peace of the countryside, and on most days, Christian would commute back home to be with his wife. In time, his successes at work afforded him the luxury of owning a modest apartment in Knightsbridge and as the years drew on he would spend more evenings there, rather than making the tiring commute back to his wife.

It was on one such fateful evening that Jessica had met Harvey's father. She had made plans to be out for dinner with friends after which they planned to go on to the cinema. They had all lost track of time and, due to their effortless nattering, would have struggled to make the film at all if Jessica had not selflessly urged them to go on ahead and get their seats while she waited at the restaurant to pay the bill. She had fully intended to catch up with them at the cinema afterwards.

Waiting at the bar, she had begun regretting her selfless decision and as she wrestled her way through her fashionably large handbag to recover her purse, she began mumbling loudly about how late she was. A rather tall gentleman, who was impatiently waiting to order himself a drink, stood helplessly watching. He painstakingly witnessed her anxiety grow more intense as she struggled to achieve anything more than to stir the contents of the bag in circles like a naïve chef hoping to save time in a cooking process by the sole act of stirring raw ingredients quickly. Looking on, the gentleman waited until he could no longer bear to witness her agony and in an act of desperation to expedite the pouring of his own potion, feeling justified in his own mind as being for her own well-being, he decided; boldly, bravely and, onlookers may have suggested stupidly, to fatefully intervene.

She had been totally preoccupied with her search and was startled by the clutch of a man's hands on her bag. Her initial reaction was to pull the bag away but the man had a steady grip and she looked up at him, her anxiety briefly turning to fear.

"How dare you?" she said looking up into his gaze and without thinking slapped him across the cheek. He paused but appeared undeterred even as the stinging sensation set in across his face. With each still holding one side of the bag, their eyes locked together and something unusual occurred. With both unsure of the intentions of the other, there appeared for several seconds to be a Mexican stand-off, neither flinching, both actually wanting to achieve the same goal.

Jessica felt an unjustified moment of regret. Confused and ashamed for lashing out, but with her bag still partly held by this stranger, she sized him up.

This is not the gaze of somebody about to do harm, she thought. The man's actions were clearly out of the ordinary and unbecoming for a gentleman. Yet he was suited like a prince. He retained a warm smile regardless of the punishment his face had just endured. His strangely inviting eyes held her in a trance and, as she stuttered on for a few moments, she unconsciously and unwillingly was lured into releasing her grip on the bag.

"Allow me," the man said in a soft but commanding tone, his eyes never leaving hers. Before Jessica had managed another word and without even setting eyes on her bag, the gentleman held out the bag in one hand and her purse in the other. Jessica was speechless. "I lose mine all of the time," he joked, and as Jessica took the purse from him, he immediately put his hand on his face to feel the warmth of his abused cheek. "I think I deserved that. May I buy you a drink?" he further enquired.

Jessica, who hadn't quite known what to say and had all but forgotten about her previous engagement, felt inexplicably drawn to this intriguing stranger and guilt ridden for lashing out at him. She coyly accepted the invitation, and that, in a nutshell, was all she had explained to Harvey.

One thing had eventually led to another and Jessica became his lover, a wife in all but marriage contract. Her life changed forever and she knowingly bore the taboo of being somebody's *other* woman from that day forward until the day of the man's untimely death.

Jessica had explained to Harvey that, this was no casual affair, but a life-long love, handicapped by poor timing and a lack of understanding by those who saw the only acceptable cessation of marriage to be one caused by death. Jessica therefore thought it further ironic that Helen would join Christian in death in the same way he had burdened her in life.

Harvey had not commented at the time, but sensed his mother was relaying her view of the relationship through heavily rose tinted glasses.

The door swung open and the receptionist simply stated,

"Mr and Mrs Walters, sir." Jessica smiled and added,

"Of differing generations." The receptionist looked past Jessica and smiled at Harvey one last time before returning to her reception.

"Please come in and sit down, the both of you." He rose from his desk and held out his hand. "I'm Michael Jones. I trust that Verity took good care of you. Damned sorry about the wait." There was a pomp within his voice. He was a scruffy but well-dressed man, a man of means yet with little time on his hands or need for the intricacies of personal presentation. His wife would shop for his suits in Savile Row and direct him to the task of attending the fittings having chosen the cloths and styles on his behalf. Worn to please, he rarely straightened his tie or checked that his shirt was neatly tucked away.

The Walters sat opposite him and watched him, with his sleeves pushed up his arms, shuffle through the mass of papers on his desk, as.

Harvey had met such people before and took an instant dislike to the man before him. He was reminded of past court rooms where criminals brought such people to defend them against crimes, which they had obviously committed. A lawyer with a warped sense that he was doing right by offering those in the wrong a fair chance at avoiding punishment for their crimes. He was not a man that would often enter Harvey's inner circle and Harvey quickly labelled him as nothing more than a *prostitute of law*.

"Well," began Mr Jones smiling across at the two of them. "We are here under rather interesting circumstances, but I am afraid my client has been unavoidably detained and won't be joining us today."

Harvey looked at the ceiling in disbelief.

"So when can we expect to meet with him?" interrupted Harvey.

"Well, that also rather depends what the purpose of the meeting is," said Mr Jones. "You see, the claim you have made of being within Mr Shaw's bloodline has come as somewhat of a shock to him, as you may imagine."

"Him and me both," responded Harvey trying not to make eye contact with his mother.

"Well, of course, and therefore at this stage in life Mr Shaw is curious as to the reason for this sudden claim. He is a man of wealth and has many enemies that may use news of your revelation for their own ends. So Mr Shaw has offered this meeting largely to forewarn you of the dangers which you may inadvertently be in should you advertise your claim publicly. And, of course, to explore what you might expect to gain etc. etc…" Mr Jones rambled on but chose to place significant emphasis on the word, "Danger".

Harvey laughed loudly in disbelief.

"Mr Jones," he said in a raised voice, "that sounds like a veiled threat."

"My son is a police officer, Mr Jones," Jessica interrupted cutting Harvey off before he had a chance to fully express his disbelief. "I am sure any such dangers would be dealt with appropriately."

The lawyer looked down and smirked at what he clearly thought to be a naive remark.

"Of course, do you mind me enquiring as to what your expectations of this meeting were?"

Harvey had not really thought this through, his motivation being more idle curiosity as to what the brother he had never had might be like rather than to consider any other consequences moving forward. However, insulted by the insinuation of less than honourable motives, he began to think that maybe he should after all have let sleeping dogs lie and in a matter of fact tone stated,

"I think we have taken up enough of your time, Mr Jones. Please apologise to my brother for this inconvenience." Without a further word Harvey gestured to his mother and made for the door.

Jessica was unusually speechless and followed Harvey closing the office door behind her. He moved at pace and was already tapping at the button to hail the elevator before Jessica caught up with him. She looked up at her son but chose to say nothing, fearing his nerves were frayed enough. They would ride the elevator back to street level before Harvey led the way in silence to the nearest café.

Meanwhile, back in the offices of *Houghton and Harrow* Michael Jones had wasted no time in making a phone call to his client.

"That's right, a policeman," he said concluding the conversation. The receptionist Verity raised an eyebrow. She had entered quietly and placed a coffee on his desk before leaving the room. There was no answer to his statement. The phone simply went quiet and Mr Jones, realising the call had been terminated by his client, replaced the handset.

Jessica chose to follow her son in silence, letting him find an empty table outside Café Rouge. She knew she had to let his mind stop spinning before she uttered any motherly words of wisdom. Without a word, she followed his lead and sat down.

"Why on earth would it put us in danger?" he voiced his thought. "Mother, what exactly have you not told me about my brother?" he asked.

"I have told you everything that happened." Jessica paused for a moment, considering what had triggered this whole episode. "I wish I had never seen that wretched article."

Harvey was taken aback. "Article? What article?" he enquired.

"It was all so long ago. I had meant to tell you about Christian years ago but the article just brought everything back." Jessica became visibly anxious. It was a Freudian slip, yet she *had* considered the article to be a minor piece of Harvey's jigsaw and given its age, she had ignored its relevance. She had naively hoped that at his stage in life, simply enlightening Harvey about her past might have been enough for him, and therefore enough for her to exonerate her conscience.

"Do you still have the magazine?" he pressed without thought for her feelings.

"Yes, yes...at home," she replied, fearing that her honest response would lead nowhere other than further anguish and heartache.

"Come on, mother," Jack said boldly standing to go. "I need to see it now." Without any further consideration, he began heading off down the street in the general direction of Jessica's apartment some twenty minute walk away.

Noticing the somewhat tense conversation taking place at their table, a waiter come over and apologetically spoke.

"Madam, I am so sorry for your wait. Is everything ok?"

Jessica had taken a tissue from her bag and was dabbing away at her eyes while getting to her feet.

"Yes, thank you. We won't be staying," she remarked awkwardly and without further ado, headed off in Harvey's direction.

Harvey was struggling to come to terms with the revelation of his brother's existence already. The lawyers meeting had done nothing but anger him and fuel his curiosity, and now there was an article too. His mind was bulging with unanswered questions.

If that hadn't been enough, he was also due to return to close protection duties the following morning during a time which he should have been sharing with his family and children following his return from the US.

Having rudely raced away from the Café Rouge, leaving his mother behind for the second time that morning, Harvey attempted to flush the multiple streams of random negative thoughts from his mind. He paused in the street, the rational side of him taking a moment to regain control before realising he had left his mother standing again. He looked back in the direction of the café and was surprised to see he had blindly travelled several hundred meters. He could only just see Jessica in the distance racing to catch up with him.

He stopped and waited. Looking back at her, he felt a deep sense of guilt for putting her through this trauma, regardless of whose fault this initially might have been. Clearly, it hadn't been an easy decision for her to make after so many years. She had been a good and loving mother throughout, and while these revelations had come as a complete shock to Harvey, nothing could take away his upbringing which, with the undivided attention of his mother, could hardly have been more pleasant.

As she approached, Harvey sighed. His sense of urgency temporarily faltering, he reached out like a lost child and wrapped his arms around his mother.

They shared each other's warmth for a moment before continuing to walk back to the apartment together. It was not a long walk and soon they found themselves back in the comfort of Jessica's home.

"It is around here somewhere," Jessica said, rummaging around magazine racks before eventually recalling its whereabouts. "I had to buy it from the surgery you know. I was quite shocked to see him after so many years, but there was simply no doubting it." She attempted to make small talk, but Harvey was not in the mood. He wasn't listening to her words, but was preoccupied with what 'danger' Mr Jones might have been referring to.

"Let me see mother," he said impatiently.

She opened at the first page of the article and handed him the magazine.

He looked down at a familiar face and smirked at the irony. "No, mother, the article about my brother..." His voice tailed off as he looked up at his mother and back down to the picture in front of him. "Oh, my God!" The words were spoken slowly and quietly as the blood drained from his face.

17 – The Last Job

It was a busy day in Exeter. Few international VIPs had toured on official visits as far from the capital as Devon. Today would be different. A high profile Bishop would visit the Cathedral as special envoy in part of an ongoing relationship building exercise between the Catholic Church and Church of England. Unusually for his level of seniority, the Bishop would require a full close protection squad which would be led on the ground by DC Harvey Walters.

It was much to the delight of the Mayor that her City of Exeter had been chosen for the high profile visit, regardless of the rumours that it was precisely the issues over protection that had led to this low profile choice of location.

Harvey's role would be to collect the Bishop and his clerical staff from Exeter airport, remain with the Bishop throughout the visit and, eventually return them all to Exeter airport. From there, they would all board a shuttle flight back to the capital and onwards back home to the Vatican the following day.

Expected to be a fairly routine, albeit rare duty, the personal protection team would return to Middlemoor for tea, cakes and the usual debriefs before being stood down and sent on their way. Harvey would then be able to return home to see out the rest of his vacation undisturbed with his family.

While he considered this job as not much more than a routine babysitting role, unworthy of his removal from a long deserved period of leave, he had nonetheless set about coordinating his team in a professional manner, utilising techniques learned from his detachment to the US where Corporate Protection roles were far more challenging.

In the few days leading up to the visit, local radio stations and press had broken their silence and stirred up curiosity towards the visit amongst the residents. The city, which housed many international students during the summer months, was expected to be crammed with those wishing to get a closer view of a dignitary from the Vatican. Many schools used the visit as an excuse for a day out of their mundane routines and children were taken down to the green in droves to offer gifts of flowers, wave flags and cheer on the Bishop's arrival.

By mid-morning on the day of the visit the Cathedral Green the streets were already teaming with students and onlookers of all ages. There was not a single table free of custom within the café's that lined the green, as the retired population took up their own strategic, yet more comfortable, viewing posts for the event.

Harvey watched as the small jet touched down on the main runway of Exeter airport. The plane would taxi across to the private hangar where he was waiting in a large British built Bentley limousine that had been driven up from London for the event. Harvey would ride out the journey into the city centre and up to the Cathedral alongside the driver who was also a part of Harvey's close protection team. The Bishop's staff would follow on behind in an array of lesser vehicles also carrying a member of Harvey's team. Once in the heart of Exeter, Harvey would escort the Bishop into the Cathedral grounds where they would be met by the Church of England dignitaries at the entrance to the Cathedral.

There would be a brief, leisurely stroll towards the Cathedral doors during which time the Bishop would be greeted by the crowds and spend several minutes, much to the delight of onlookers, talking in Italian, Spanish, English and French to those foreign students who greeted him. Photographers would get their opportunity to click away at the representatives of the two churches standing together, all bearing smiles, at the entrance of the Cathedral after the greetings had taken place. Or such was the brief to Harvey and from Harvey to his team.

As the Bishop actually approached the steps to the Cathedral, a young girl crouched under the rope that stretched the length of the street to hold onlookers back. Harvey, realising she was no threat, kept a watchful eye, but allowed this minor breach in security to take place. She reached out and spoke to the Bishop in full view of the grateful reporters who swarmed around the scene clicking away furiously as the girl handed him a single red rose. He lifted the rose to smell its scent and, seemingly delighted with this small gift, chose to hold on to it in his left hand while offering her a special blessing for her kind act. Photographers were delighted at this unplanned scene and, sensing a headline picture, jostled for position to get the best shots.

There were flashes from the cameras of journalists and overjoyed onlookers alike. The crowds cheered and applauded as the Bishop made his way up the steps leading to the Cathedral entrance.

One man who wasn't smiling was Jack Shaw. He had been watching the Bishop's arrival intensely from an apartment above the Half a Nickel Tea Rooms.

Looking through his telescopic sight he had observed as one man stood by the passenger side of the limousine speaking into his lapel microphone. He held what Jack guessed to be a small earpiece tightly against his ear so that he could hear the voices of his colleagues above the noise of the amassed crowds. He took one final look around before assisting the Bishop from the vehicle.

Jack had been visibly shaken. He looked up and away from his rifle momentarily. He had seen the Bishop being led from the car by a man he had come to know as *Bill Moore*, an underworld thief from Detroit. While he had only met Bill on two occasions, he was convinced this was *definitely* one and the same man. Moreover, this left Jack with an incredible and untimely dilemma. He made a quick sweep of the area through his sights to see if there were any other unplanned surprises he should be aware of, but he could see nothing further out of the ordinary.

His mind digested the information and Jack inadvertently missed the first planned opportunity of taking on the hit for which he was there. *Bill Moore was a mole for the British government?* he thought. There was only one possible course of action for Jack to take.

Jack looked down the barrel of his rifle through the sight and down to the cross hairs. He focussed in on the

Bishop and then on the man standing next to him. He paused, his mind racing through the possible outcomes of a major plan deviation. A man of his expertise *could* take both individuals out within a couple of seconds, though the second shot would be taken through the mayhem that the first shot would cause.

A clean and defining shot to first take out the single close protection officer known to him as Bill Moore should leave him a clear yet brief opportunity to take out his bountied target as the crowd scattered. He paused for thought before looking back down the sight.

He began regulating his breathing as he had done so many times before. *Inhale slowly, exhale slightly, hold and squeeze the trigger.* The words of The Phoenix drummed into his mind during an intense period of training raced through his mind. *"Exhale slightly moments before pulling the trigger to allow your body to relax, Jack. This will vastly reduce any chance of judder or shake,"* The Phoenix would say.

The sights lined up, it was time for that one last slow and deep intake of breath. Leaving his main kill for a second shot would be a risky undertaking and there would be no time to pause for breath. He would be relying upon all of his skills and concentration to take it on successfully.

Jack Shaw was about to take a decision that no other would have. In his mind, he could picture the glory of a successful double hit. His self-confidence was peaking. *Is this misguided confidence?* he thought. He could not, must not believe nor consider his plan to fail.

His mind computed the outcomes one last time. A single bead of sweat appeared upon his brow. At worst, the Bishop would attempt to run for cover, but he would not outrun a bullet of The Phoenix. At best he would hit the floor on seeing the first man down, making himself a sitting duck. Slowly, Jack began to exhale and with his mind made up, his finger waited on the trigger.

Jack squeezed down and an unlikely event he had not considered was already occurring. His intense concentration was marred by the voice of an intruder shouting indistinctly from behind him. The shot rang out and Jack's lightning reactions sent his body swerving around to meet the intruder. Looking straight into his eyes and without pausing for thought he shot again, this time from the hip.

"What the fuck?" was all Joe could muster before he hit the ground.

Jack swung back around to the window. Immediately adopting a firing position he looked through the sights to see his first target lying motionless on the ground. People were beginning to swarm around him to witness his fate, but then Jack felt the pit of his stomach tightened as he observed his primary target being shuffled into his limousine. There would be no second shot.

Joe Collier had unwittingly saved the life of Jack's target to his own detriment. Jack quickly and expertly dismantled his weapon, wiping it down as he did so, before returning it to its case. On his way towards the door he gave an angry kick to the ribs of the deceased man lying on the floor in front of him.

"Asshole!" he muttered under his breath and left the room.

He didn't like unforeseen events but had become accustomed to dealing with them. They never seemed to faze him, a trait which over the years had lulled him into almost believing he was invincible. But today was different. The target had got away and he had not earned his bounty. Jack's first shot had been lucky. The intrusion had put him off balance but he had witnessed Bill Moore lying motionless on the ground.

Amidst the chaos that ensued down at the green, Jack was alone in his composure. He would slip away down to the river Exe where he would dispose of his weapon in the river before making his way discreetly from the city centre and on towards Marsh Barton Industrial Estate. He would crew up with workers from a removals company travelling east for a job. The business was one of many Lucio owned and, to the crew, Jack would just be a temp making up numbers. He would discreetly disappear during a rest stop at Chievely Services and make his own way back to his home. Once there, he would lay low for a few days before flying back to his wife by private jet.

The authorities would be taken aback by this event. Yet for all the planning in the world, on that day; they would be unable to stop this lone assassin from walking away, scot free.

Back in Exeter, it seemed that for hours, all that could be heard were the noise of sirens, screams of disbelieving children and clicking of photographers eager to record this fateful day for the city.

Harvey Walters aka Bill Moore remained motionless and not breathing when emergency services arrived on the scene. Attempts at resuscitation continued while he was rushed by ambulance through the streets of Exeter and on to the Accident and Emergency department of the RD & E Hospital.

The Bishop had not flinched during the brief and deadly encounter. Standing like a bird blinded by the headlights of a car, a statue, seemingly in acceptance of any fate that his good Lord desired. The only thing suggesting he wasn't stuck in time, was the rose that had been presented to him some moments earlier which, having escaped the grasp of his left hand, appeared to float as though weightless until it eventually reached its resting place on the ground.

Following the shot, he had been quickly manhandled into his vehicle by the driver who sped away from the scene to a secret location. Police escorts in pursuit, while the authorities tried to get a handle on what had just taken place.

The city was locked down by emergency services but this was largely a matter of process. There was no indication of who or what they were looking for. They could only go through the motions in the hope that blind luck would intervene and offer them a useful lead but, blind luck was simply not on the side of the authorities that day.

18 – The Letter

Harvey Walters sat next to his bed. Jenny, Chloe and Rob were due to arrive any moment to take him home. His mother would not be with them, instead choosing to wait for her family at their home.

She would organise a welcome home spread and spent most of that sunny morning erecting bunting outside the house much to the curiosity of the neighbours on their small estate.

Some of Harvey's more friendly neighbours had been invited to come around for a drink and to welcome the hero home. Greg Bickley would be there along with other colleagues from his workplace.

Harvey was unaware that he would later that year receive a promotion for the perceived heroism in saving the Bishop's life. Only he and one other really knew what had happened on that fateful day and for Harvey, while he would in time make a full recovery thanks to the keen and watchful eyes of Nurse Stevens and Doctor Stone, the episode was still somewhat of a blur.

The recovery process in the Royal Devon & Exeter Hospital had lasted several weeks before doctors would allow him to leave the hospital. Even during this relatively brief period, Harvey had shown signs of ageing quite substantially, his body expressing its disgust at being put through such an ordeal. His hair showed signs of greying and while he had regained his humorous outward personality, his eyes would portray deep inner pain.

That morning the hospital staff had gathered the numerous cards that had flooded into the hospital during the days after Harvey had been shot. Well-wishers from all over had taken time out to purchase gifts and send them on with their prayers for his speedy recovery. All those that left contact addresses would in time receive notes of thanks from Harvey as he continued to convalesce at home with his family.

The noise of excited children could be heard and Harvey's gaze was broken, a smile quickly transformed him from deep thoughts back into the real world.

Chloe and Rob appeared and ran the final few metres as he held open his arms to embrace them. Despite the fruitless calls of Jenny for them to be careful with their fragile father, they launched at him to hold him tight after what had been the second long, and this time unplanned, separation from their father.

Jenny stood by smiling and watching until the children finally allowed Harvey a moment to embrace his wife. In turn she would embrace Harvey, more gently yet with equal passion, before they took stock to gather his belongings and medication and make their way out of the ward.

Harvey had already spoken to Nurse Stevens and Dr Stone that morning, during which time he had expressed his warmest thanks and gratitude for their help during his recovery. He was not expecting any further goodbyes.

As they were exiting the ward a voice called from behind them.

"Mr Walters, Mr Walters, one moment please." It was an auxiliary nurse who was waiving an envelope in her hand. Harvey faced the nurse and she continued, "I'm sorry, Mr Walters, but you wouldn't want to leave without this," she exclaimed holding out the envelope and looking across to smile at Jenny.

"More forms?" Harvey enquired paying little attention but still managing a smile.

"No," replied the nurse. "It's a telegram, it arrived this morning for you but the sender only put the main hospital address, so we've been searching all over for you." She looked somewhat out of breath but proud to have at last found the rightful owner of the envelope.

"Thank you," replied Harvey and gave her his customary smile before turning to Jenny and continuing down the corridor.

"Well, aren't you going to open it?" Jenny asked. "After all they've been looking all over the hospital for you," she giggled.

Harvey looked at the postmark. His eyebrows raised as he noted this was from overseas. He tore at the envelope. The contents read as follows:

Harvey,

I apologise for missing you at our recent meeting. Let me assure you that I won't miss you again given another opportunity.

Your brother,
Jack Shaw.

"Well, that's good news, isn't it?" Jenny said looking over his shoulder with a beaming smile. "He does want to meet with you after all."

Harvey stopped. He looked visibly startled and whispered quietly,
"Perhaps…" His eyes hovered over the innuendo within the text and he felt a chill run down his spine.

"Are you okay, Harvey?" asked Jenny.

He stuffed the letter in his trouser pocket deciding to re-examine it later. Looking back to Jenny he buried his thoughts and regained his composure before replying,

"Of course. Come on, let's go home."

THE END.